WITCH APPEAL

A MAGICAL RENOVATION MYSTERY BOOK ELEVEN

AMY BOYLES

LADYBUGBOOKS, LLC

Witch Appeal

AMY BOYLES

CHAPTER 1

$\mathcal{M}$y name is Clementine Cooke. I'm a witch in a heaping amount of big trouble.

"Be prepared. The cloud's coming," Rufus Mayes, my boyfriend, told us.

Jack, a person who up until about five seconds before I had thought was nothing more than a homeless man, raised his staff. He pointed it at the mason jar he held. The lid unscrewed and flew up into the wind that was slapping me in the face.

Magical orbs bounced inside the canister, but they didn't unleash into the wind.

"Clem, I'm scared," yelled my furry dachshund, Lady. "Hold me!"

"Not now," I told her. "Run up onto Malene's porch. Head for cover."

From the porch, Malene, Urleen and Norma Ray tromped down, looking like the three witches of Eastwick about fifty years later.

"It's a magical storm," Malene informed us.

I had guessed as much. We'd only just recently learned that our town, Peachwood, was being targeted by a group of people known as clearers. Several centuries ago they had scoured the land in search of witches in what had become known as the Great Clearing.

Only a few weeks earlier, a clearer had come to our town and killed two of our kind, pretending the whole while to be a friend. That was when we learned that clearers themselves had magic. They wanted to be some sort of sick heroes to humans, convince them that witches were evil and that the clearers were good. But in reality they wanted to reset the magical world in their own image, the way that they wanted it to be seen.

Well, my family and I weren't about to let that happen. Whatever was pushing this storm, they were about to face off against…one homeless man who looked a little on the crazy side, my boyfriend who used to be consumed by darkness, me, a scared dachshund and three old women, one of whom needed glasses and refused to wear them.

Yep. This was the team that would lead the world into battle against the apocalypse.

Or we would decide to sit and enjoy finger sandwiches instead.

Malene was beside me now. "What orbs do you have?" she said to Jack.

He frowned into the jar. "I've got an ice spell, a sneezing orb, two bottomless pit spells—be careful of those—and a jalapeno pepper spell."

"Jalapeno pepper?" I asked.

He nodded soberly. "Makes your mouth burn so bad that you won't be able to cast a spell for weeks."

I shot Rufus a *help us* look. "Everyone," he said, "spread out. I'm going to hit the cloud with everything I have."

We did as Rufus said. He threw out his arms, and for some reason we all copied him. Lightning flashed and crackled as the dark cloud rolled straight for us.

Rufus grimaced as the air became electrified. The ozone smell thickened, and the hairs on the backs of my arms rose. I realized too late what he was doing.

Lightning bounced off his skin. He was supercharging himself with the intention of throwing all the power back at the cloud in the hopes of breaking it apart.

"Stop!" The fierce wind grabbed my words and tossed them away. "It's too much power. You'll hurt yourself!"

"I can do it," he ground out. Sweat poured down his forehead. His skin was bubbling from the exertion. "I've got this."

"No, you don't!" To Jack, I shouted, "Hit the cloud with whatever you can. All of you!"

Jack threw every orb he had at the cloud. Malene, Urleen and Norma Ray put their hands together, and a super orb appeared between them.

It was so close now that I could feel what it was. The roiling darkness wasn't just made of atmospheric gas; it was evil incarnate. There was no hope, no goodness in it. Inside there was only misery and defeat. If it rained on Peachwood, all that sadness would be released onto the people of my town. It would become infectious, and when the clearers arrived, the humans would easily hand the witches and wizards over.

We would have lost before this battle ever even began.

Not heeding Rufus's command, I grabbed hold of his arm and nearly fainted. An electric current ran through my body, jarring me to the point that I couldn't think straight. My teeth chattered and Rufus glanced over at me, his eyes begging me to let go.

It was too late now. I was glued to him. Even if I'd wanted to release him, the force of the current had suctioned me to his body.

"Release on three," he told me.

How was he even talking? I could barely remember my own name.

"One…"

My head felt like it was about to burst.

"Two…"

I thought my skin was going to melt off the bone.

"Three!"

I don't know how I did it, but I released every bit of power that I had. Rufus took it and aimed the magic straight at the cloud.

The magic formed a golden javelin that looked to be ten yards long and thick as a man's arm. The pointy end pierced the cloud. Lightning and thunder illuminated the cloud where it touched. The cloud rumbled and the electricity inside it flickered as the javelin moved down the length of the gaseous beast.

The entire sky flared bright, and for a brief second I thought all was lost. The bottom of the cloud became deep purple, and I just knew the rain was about to unleash.

But then, just like that, the cloud erupted from the inside and ripped apart.

I started to exhale. But before I could relax too deeply, the cloud made the face of a man. He had a chiseled brow and deep parentheses on either side of his mouth.

I am coming for you, Clementine, he said.

I blinked to make sure that I was truly seeing what I believed. But before I could get my wits about me, the face vanished.

"Did you see that?" I asked Rufus.

"You going against my wishes?"

I scowled. "No. The face."

"What face?"

"In the cloud." I pointed toward it. "Up there, before it disintegrated."

He eyed me skeptically, one perfectly dark brow arched. "Are you feeling all right?"

I swatted away Rufus's hand as he reached to check my forehead's temperature. "I'm feeling fine. No. I saw it. A face."

"If you saw it, it was only meant for you to witness."

It took a moment to digest that. The face that had appeared was only meant for me. Why? What had I done to deserve such torment? Why was it wanting to deal with me and me alone?

Perhaps I was jumping the gun. Maybe it was just my imagination.

But as I headed inside, there was no doubt in my mind that what I'd seen had been real. But what was it, and why had it appeared?

IN MALENE's HOUSE, we quickly went into battle/high alert mode. "Everyone"—Rufus clapped his hands—"what did you sense out there?"

"Great evil." Jack sniffed, wiped his nose on his sleeve. "That was only a taste of the power that's coming here, to hurt this town. We've got to be prepared."

"The last time we tried to prepare folks for battle, people died," Malene reminded us. "Our meetings were taken advantage of by Champ. If we called one now, there would be no telling how many unrecognizable faces we would see."

"Witches and wizards would come out of the woodwork," Norma Ray agreed.

"Say they're from neighboring towns." Urleen pulled her cardigan tight to her neck. "They'd claim to be one of us, but they could be clearers. There'd be no way to know if they were telling the Lord's honest truth or if they were just fibbing."

"Fibbing," Norma Ray said with a hard nod. "No doubt about it."

Rufus patted the air with both hands. "Before we start making assumptions, we need to base things on fact."

"Fact," Lady said, "a huge cloud tried to kill us. Fact, we barely escaped with our lives."

Willard Gandy came out from the kitchen. "Now, Lady. You made it safe and sound. You all did thanks to everyone's talents."

As we talked, the truth hit me in a wave. "There's no point having a plan because we don't know who the enemy is and when they'll strike. We're lost at sea in this. We don't have a target."

"Not yet we don't," Rufus pointed out. "But the evil is coming. We've got to be able to recognize it when it surfaces. If not, we're all doomed."

Everyone was quiet for a moment. It was Malene who spoke. "What do we look for?"

"There will be newcomers," Jack said, almost in a trancelike state. Actually he *was* in a trance. His irises and pupils had vanished, leaving pale white eyeballs to stare out from his head. "There will be three, and it will be difficult to know who is friend and who is foe. They will all show up at once. They will all be respected and believed. Friend will be foe, and foe will be friend. The one who is thought to be evil will be good and the good will be evil."

"What?" Norma Ray said.

"He's talking about a wolf in sheep's clothing," Urleen whispered behind her hand, loud enough to wake the dead.

"Oh, I get it. What else?" she asked Jack. His eyes returned to their normal state, and she said, "Well, I guess that's it."

Jack's hand shot out and grabbed her shoulder. Norma Ray screamed. His eyes had gone white again.

Well, I supposed that *wasn't* it, after all.

"You must all be careful," he continued. "The fates will be against you. The tide of the town will turn from you. You will be lost, alone. At your weakest moment, you will be strongest."

He went quiet and all of us leaned in. Would he speak again?

"And then," Jack's voice boomed, and Norma Ray jumped, "the reckoning will come."

The room filled with silence. I held my breath, waiting. But Jack's eyes returned to normal, and he patted his belly. "Oh, man, am I hungry. Why're y'all staring at me?"

"You went into a trance," Rufus explained. "Prophecy came from your mouth."

Jack scratched his face in confusion. "Oh, that happened? Been a while since I've done any of that talking. Did you learn anything good?"

Malene huffed. "Only that our friends will be enemies, and that three people who will be highly respected will come to town. That's what we got. You care to shed some light on things?"

"I can't." Jack folded his arms and surveyed us. "When I get one of my spells, I don't know what I'm saying. The words just come out. But I can tell you, I've never been wrong."

Norma Ray quirked a brow skeptically. "How can you be so sure if you don't know what you're saying?"

"I just am," he told her flatly.

They stared each other down, and I was certain Norma Ray was about to throw punches (if she could have figured out exactly where Jack's face was due to her impaired eyesight), when Rufus spoke.

"Everyone, there is much to be done. We may be hampered in terms of knowledge, but Jack has just given us golden pearls of wisdom. We must be on the lookout. Anyone new comes to town, we report it to one another. We keep eyes on Peachwood."

"For all we know, the people are already here," Willard said soberly.

"Exactly. So we must be vigilant. People can be coaxed to the wrong side."

We nodded, silently agreeing to spy on our town, on our friends or neighbors. If they knew of anyone new to Peachwood or were seen talking with someone that we didn't recognize, we'd have to investigate.

Because our friends could end up serving the darkness, whether they intended to or not.

And for that, we all needed to be wary—every one of us.

CHAPTER 2

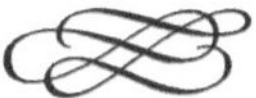

The next day I took Lady for a walk downtown. The fur on her back was erect, and my dog was on edge, alert.

"I'm gonna find out who this traitor is," she said.

I bit back a laugh. "Lady, we're not looking for a traitor. We're looking to see who's new in town."

"Same thing," she told me, eyes peeled wide.

The truth was, there were so many people in town that I didn't recognize most of them. The economy had exploded of late, and an influx of newcomers had arrived from all over the country. The entire continent was experiencing a massive shift in migration, which meant plenty of folks had come this way.

So perhaps I wasn't the best person to judge who was new and who wasn't. Tired of spying a swarm of new faces and with no clue how to decipher who was bad and who was good, I said, "Let's grab a cup of coffee."

"Great. I could use a blueberry muffin. How does that sound?"

"Sounds like it'll upset your stomach."

Lady lifted her nose proudly. "If that's the worst thing it does, I can deal with it. You've got to enjoy life, Clem. Eat chocolate, enjoy rich foods. When you're on your deathbed, do you really think that you're going to be glad that you didn't indulge in order to keep your figure?"

"First of all, I do indulge. I eat chocolate every day."

"Oh, that is true. Well, I'll just save my talk for someone else, then."

Bender's Coffee was packed. Julie, the owner, was busy manning the cash register. She smiled when our gazes met.

"Clem, this is just about the busiest we've ever been. I've had to hire more help."

My ears perked up at that. "Really?" I glanced over her shoulder and spied a new girl working the espresso machine. She looked harmless enough—fresh out of high school with her ebony hair pulled back into a sleek ponytail and a smattering of freckles across her nose. "Hi there!"

She glanced over. "Hey."

"That's Trina. Trina, meet Clem. She'll have a hot mocha."

"You know me too well," I replied with a smile to Julie.

"I do, and I don't have time to dillydally today. We're slammed." She glanced over the counter at Lady. "But I do have some dog treats that I made up—peanut butter bones. You think she wants one?"

Lady drooled. "Yes, I think she wants one," I told Julie.

I paid and moved down the counter to feel Trina out. Could she be in town to destroy all the witches and wizards?

"So, you're new?" I asked, trying to establish a friendly not-being-nosy tone.

"Yep." Trina cleaned the milk foaming spout with a towel. "Arrived a few weeks ago." She winked at me. "There's something special about this town. I think you know what I mean. After all, your company is called Magical Renovations, right?"

"Yes. Yes it is," I said slowly, wrapping my head around her meaning. "The key word being magical."

"I agree." Trina leaned over. "By the way, I don't know anyone here. Do you think that you could introduce me to some folks who are, you know, like us?"

"I sure can," I nearly shouted. "I have a grandmother who would love to meet you. And she has several friends who would also love to meet you."

"Great. It's always hard being new in town."

"Yes, I'd love to know what brought you here." *And what plans you have to destroy Peachwood.* "Let me give you my number."

She gave me her digits, and I texted her with a quick message. Trina made my coffee and I grabbed that, as well as Lady's snack, and we headed out.

As soon as we were outside, Lady said, "You thinking what I'm thinking?"

"Yep," I said, talking about Trina.

"That this doggie treat is going to be the best ever?"

I didn't hold back a laugh even though folks glanced at me, eyes questioning what had given me a chuckle. I quickly glanced down at my phone and laughed again. Lady was great at keeping her voice low, and I didn't want to draw attention to the fact that she could talk.

We had enough problems on our hands already.

I gave her the treat, and she swallowed it in one bite. "Well, I guess it was good," I murmured.

"Best." She licked her chops. "Ever."

With that, we headed home.

"She's a solid lead," I told Malene a little while later. "New to town and asking a lot about magic."

Malene turned off her mixer, where a dark, rich, chocolaty batter swam in the bowl. "I don't like it. This clearer, I think it's going to be a man."

"Now that's just sexist," Lady said. "Or genderist. I cain't keep up with the lingo nowadays. But what I'm saying is, evil can come in the form of a woman."

Malene pointed to the batter. "Help me lift this bowl, will you?"

I did as she said, holding it while she pulled the bowl over two round and floured cake pans. "Will you meet her?"

Malene licked chocolate from her fingers. "I'll meet her, but I don't think she's the one."

The face that I'd seen in the cloud had certainly been masculine. But it could have been that way to trick me. "She could be wearing a glamour to throw us off the scent."

My grandmother considered this. "Very true. Fine. Invite her to Sunday lunch tomorrow. We'll poke and prod her. It'll be just us ladies."

"What about Rufus and Willard?"

She tsked. "Yes, they would want to meet her. But you can't have roosters in a henhouse."

"Not unless you want all the hens to wind up pregnant," Lady informed us.

What a delightful thought.

~

THE NEXT MORNING WAS SUNDAY, which meant church, so I dressed in a simple green dress with a belt and pointy-toed pumps.

"You look nice," Lady told me as I admired my reflection in the mirror.

The dress was perfect, highlighting the cinch at my waist (which wouldn't stay cinched if I kept only eating chocolate for breakfast) and complimenting my skin tone and hair color nicely. It was new and this was the first chance that I'd had to show it off. A date night with Rufus would've been a good chance to don it, too, but with everything that had been going on, our dating life was taking a hit.

Rufus was so busy trying to figure out what the clearers had planned that he was wrapped up in research. It was fine. Everything would return to normal once we discovered who the bad guys were and we saved the magical people in our town from succumbing to a fate worse than death.

Or so I hoped.

As I pushed a pair of emerald studs into my ears, the doorbell rang.

Lady barked, "Intruder alert! Intruder! Stay back, Clem. This could be the bad guy."

I laughed. "First of all, the person isn't actually inside, so they're not an intruder. Secondly, it's only Willard. He's come to pick me up for church."

"What if the person's only pretending to be Willard?" She sprang to the window, scratching at the sheers to move them out of her way. "What if it's really a sea monster, come to drag you to the depths of the ocean?"

"Um, that's a risk I'm willing to take." I opened the door to find Willard standing on my porch. His hair was combed neatly to one side, and he was freshly shaven. He greeted me with a kiss on the cheek and a low whistle.

"You look beautiful. Is this a special occasion?"

I laughed and waved him away. "No, just a new dress."

"Well, you'll be the prettiest girl in all of church."

A horn honked from the street. Malene stuck her head out of the passenger window of Willard's truck. "Let's get a move on! Church will start without us, and I got to get a good seat."

"Why's she in such a rush?" I asked.

Willard rolled his eyes. "This week's sermon is on atoning for your sins. She wants to see who all shows up, and stare them down."

I bit back a laugh. "Sounds about right. Let me just grab my purse and we'll head out."

"I thought that I was going to have to send in the National Guard," Malene said when I slid onto the back seat of the truck. "What took y'all so long?"

"For your information," Willard said, "I was complementing our granddaughter on how nice she looked."

Malene pulled down the visor and opened the cosmetic mirror. She stared at me and nodded. "Nice dress. I like it. Maybe I can borrow it sometime."

Malene was a good foot shorter than me, and so I didn't think the gown would be a good fit. But I wasn't about to burst her bubble.

"Sure. You can borrow it any time you want."

"Thank you. Now, Willard. Let's get to church."

Apparently the atonement sermon was a popular one. The First Baptist Church of Peachwood's parking lot was bursting at the seams. It looked as busy as Easter services. The weather was warm, and all the women were in their Sunday finest—high heels and colorful skirts and dresses. The hues reflected early summer—bright pinks, vibrant blues, seafoam green.

The inside of the church was just as busy as the outside, with people milling about holding disposable coffee cups that they'd gotten from one of the several self-serve stations that were sprinkled around the building.

Children were being taken to their Sunday programs by mothers while husbands and fathers stood around, chatting before it was time for the service to start.

"Would either of you ladies like some coffee?" Willard asked.

"I would," I told him.

"Malene?"

She shook her head. "No, I need to get inside. Come on, Clem. Willard will catch up to us."

We left him in the hall and headed in. The sanctuary was a beautiful room filled with sparkling light that streamed through a single stained glass rose window that stood behind the pulpit and above the choir.

Many of the seats were already filled, and I had the feeling that Malene wouldn't get the front-row pew that she wanted.

"Malene! Clem! Over here!"

Norma Ray stood in the second row waving us over. "Oh, let's go," Malene told me.

We made our way through the crowd and reached Norma Ray, who sat with Urleen. They had saved half a pew, though I spotted several people eyeing it as they searched for their own places to sit.

"I'm so glad you're here," Norma Ray said. "Urleen was about to get into a fight over your seats."

"I was not," Urleen snapped.

Norma Ray rolled her eyes and mouthed, *Yes, she was.*

Urleen spoke. "I was just telling Claire Rose that we were saving these."

Norma Ray glanced over her shoulder. "That was when Claire asked if it was more Christian to give the seats to someone who was present, as opposed to someone who wasn't. And do you know what Urleen said?"

"What?" I asked, dropping my purse on the bench.

"She said"—Norma Ray chuckled—"that all of us believe in someone we can't see—Jesus—and so she believed that Malene would be along any minute."

Malene nodded. "I bet that shut Claire up."

"It sure did. I told Urleen that everyone in town would know what she'd done by tomorrow."

"This afternoon, I believe," Urleen replied.

Willard joined us and handed me the coffee. We'd just sat when the lights dimmed and the band started playing. We rose and sang several praise songs before the lights came up and the pastor stepped out.

But it wasn't Pastor Steve, like it usually was. Instead a completely different pastor stood in his place. He looked like an angel with light hair and a big smile.

"Sorry for the surprise," he announced. "But Pastor Steve couldn't be here today. My name is Pastor Clark, and I thank y'all for welcoming me to First Baptist."

CHAPTER 3

For the next forty minutes I was completely distracted. All I could think about was that we had a new, unannounced pastor. He just up and appeared. Where was Steve? What had happened to him?

All of it was much too suspicious.

As soon as the very last song ended and we were dismissed, Malene shot out of her seat.

"Where is he? Where's the imposter?"

Willard placed a hand on Malene's shoulder. "I know what you're thinking, but there's no way that the clearers—"

"There *is* a way." She poked the air in defiance. "What better means to hide the devil than to put him in a sheepskin?"

Willard looked over at me. "Clem, would you talk some sense into your grandmother?"

I hated to tell Willard, but Malene had the same thought as me. I was two seconds away from pinching the pastor to see if he'd turn evil.

"Let's go meet him," Malene said. "Come on, girls."

Willard begrudgingly stepped aside and let the four of us out of the pew. When Malene wanted to, she could fly like the wind, and fly we did. We raced to the exit, standing in line as others waited to shake hands with Pastor Clark.

Claire was right in front of us. She wore a hat with buttery silk roses pinned to it and a simple pink dress that matched. It was quite a pretty outfit; too bad the woman inside of it ruined it.

"I see you made it, Malene," Claire quipped. "For a while there, I thought that I was going to have to steal your seat."

Malene frowned. "Happy Lord's day to you, too, Claire."

"Did I say something wrong? You know how filled up the church is on atonement day."

"I see you attended," Malene fired back. "Have a lot of sins to atone for?" She wiggled her brows in suggestion. "Any that I need to know about?"

"Sins that I have?" Claire brushed hair from her face using a withered hand. One of hers was completely normal, but the other was smaller, shrunken. Claire had told us that she'd been born that way—a genetic defect. "I would ask the same of you, since you made sure to sit up front."

Norma Ray interjected. "Oh, everyone knows all about Malene's sins. She drives over the speed limit and has a tendency to jaywalk."

Claire rolled her eyes. "Yes, I'm sure that's all."

Malene's hands flew to her hips. "Just what are you suggesting? That I'm some big fat *pink* sinner?"

Malene's gaze flitted to Claire's hat, and Claire's jaw dropped. "Why, I'm no more a sinner than you, Malene Fredericks, and you need to remember that."

"Really? What about all those men I hear have been going into and out of your house recently?"

At that, Claire's mouth slammed shut and she turned around to wait her turn in silence.

Malene snickered and winked at me as if to say, *I got the best of her, didn't I?*

I supposed she had, but it was never good to air anyone's dirty laundry in public, no matter how nasty they were to you.

Why was it that I had to teach my own grandmother the rules of life? I sighed and tapped my foot, hoping the line would move faster. The heels I wore weren't completely broken in yet, and they pinched my toes.

I shifted my weight and glanced down at the heels. When I looked up, I had a clear view of Pastor Clark. Closer than we'd been in the sanctuary, I could make out that his creamy skin was flawless. So were his shining teeth when he pulled his lips back into a smile.

He cupped Claire's hand gently and introduced himself. He repeated her name back to her after she said it, and they chatted for a few seconds, Claire gushing about what a wonderful sermon it was, and that she was glad that he'd kept to the topic of atonement. She sneaked a quick glance back at Malene, who scowled.

Then Claire walked off and it was our turn.

"Thank you for coming," Clark said. "I hope my sermon didn't bore you."

"It did not." Malene pushed herself right up to him. "My name is Malene Fredericks. This is my granddaughter, Clementine, and my friends Urleen and Norma Ray."

He repeated everyone's name, and before he had a chance to say anything else, Malene blurted out, "Where's Steve?"

"He was called out of town unexpectedly. His mother is sick, and he took his whole family to visit." Clark smiled at all of us. "I hope I was a decent replacement."

"You were a lot prettier to look at," Norma Ray informed him. "I'm sure Clem would say so, too, but she has a boyfriend."

I wanted to die.

"And what of your family?" Malene wiggled her brows. "Where are they?"

"Ah, alas, but I'm not married." Clark placed a hand to his chest. "I'm still searching for my perfect wife."

"Well, don't search too hard for perfection," Urleen added, "because we know it doesn't exist in us humans."

"That it does not," Clark agreed. "Well, thank you for coming."

"Will you be around long?" Malene asked.

"Yes, for maybe a week or two. I plan to take up Pastor Steve's duties, visiting and preaching."

"Then we'll be seeing you," Malene said.

Clark smiled. "Yes, I would like that."

We walked on, leaving the parishioners behind us to chat with the young pastor. Malene glanced over her shoulder at me and scowled.

I knew what she was thinking—that we had our man. But to be honest, I wasn't quite so sure.

∽

"How was church?" Rufus asked when he called me later.

"Great. We missed you."

"You think folks miss having a man in leather pants attend services?"

"Yeah," I joked, "it would be like having a rock god in attendance. Folks would love it."

He chuckled. "Far be it from me to deny the people what they want."

I laughed aloud at that. "I know. You'll have to come sometime."

"Perhaps."

Though Rufus was part of my life in pretty much every other area, church was something that he skipped. Maybe it was because of his dark past and he didn't think he'd ever be accepted. I'd told him before that everyone was forgiven in God's eyes, but he still didn't come with me.

But one of these day I was going to whittle down his resolve to a nub.

"We had a new pastor today," I said.

His tone perked up at that. "Tell me everything." So I did, mentioning how Pastor Steve was suddenly called away and Clark took his place. When I finished, he asked, "What do you think of him? Do you believe him to be someone worth investigating?"

"I'm not sure. But Malene thinks so."

"Of course she does," he said without missing a beat. "I wouldn't expect anything less."

"Which reminds me, I need to get going. She's having a newcomer to town over for lunch. Her name's Trina and she works at Bender's."

"I've seen her."

"You have? Why haven't you mentioned her to me?"

"Well, I suppose because I've been trying to figure out who could be the one coming to destroy us all, and I haven't wanted to simply start pointing fingers at people who may or may not be guilty."

"Oh, you mean, you don't want to jump the gun like Malene?"

"No, I don't." He sighed. "Keep me abreast of how things go, and if the pastor stays around, let me know that, too."

"Aye, aye, captain."

I could imagine Rufus rolling his eyes. "All right. Let's not be dramatic. Talk to you soon."

We got off the phone, and I headed over to Malene's, having changed into a pair of jeans and a silky blouse.

I arrived just as Trina was pulling up. "Thank you for inviting me," she said. "I'm so glad you're here at the same time. I hate going into places all alone."

"I know exactly what you mean. Come on. You'll love Malene." Perhaps *love* was too strong a word. "I mean, you'll definitely like my grandmother."

Trina shot me a worried look. "Why? Is something wrong with her?"

"No, no. Of course not." I laughed as if that was the silliest thing I'd ever heard. Which it absolutely wasn't. "No. She's very welcoming, just maybe a little rough around the edges at times."

I knocked on the front door, and Malene appeared wearing a pair of bright pink leggings and an oversize white T-shirt. "Well, look who it is —Clem, and this must be the new friend Trina that you've told me about." She pulled Trina into a ferocious hug. "Oh, you smell so good— like vanilla. Let me get a good look at you. Well, aren't you the cutest witch I've seen in ages? Come on in and meet the girls."

Norma Ray and Urleen were in the living, standing against the wall, waiting to meet Trina.

And they were wearing matching pink leggings and white shirts. What was going on? Had I stepped into an episode of *The Twilight Zone*?

"Y'all," Malene said to them, "this is Trina."

"How do you do?" Urleen took her hand. "So nice to meet you."

"I'm doing well, thank you." She looked over her shoulder at me and smiled as if to say, *They're all so nice. What were you talking about, prickly?*

Norma Ray stepped forward. "Now, we're going to be on our best behavior because Malene said that if we weren't, she'd feed us orbs that made us fart."

The room went silent. It was Urleen who laughed. "Norma Ray, what are you talking about? Nothing like that happened."

Norma Ray withered. Sometimes her inner voice became her outer voice. I didn't think she knew when thinking turned into speaking.

Malene took Trina's hand. "Come on, dear. I've got everything set up. Would you like some tea? Lemonade?"

"Lemonade would be nice, thank you."

We all sat and Malene served us chicken casserole topped with crushed Ritz crackers and frozen cranberry salad. We ate in silence for a moment before Malene spoke.

"Trina, tell us what brings you to Peachwood."

"Well"—she wiped her mouth with a napkin—"I had heard about this town, that there's a thriving witch population, and I wanted to come see it and be a part of it. Where I'm from, there aren't any witches."

"Well, there are plenty of us here." Malene pointed to Urleen and Norma Ray. "So you're definitely in good company."

"What I wonder"—Trina lowered her fork—"is how the human population deals with the magic?"

Norma Ray's brows lifted. In fact, I think all our brows did. "How the humans deal with it?"

"Yes, I mean, do they accept witches and wizards? Is there any tension in the relationship?"

"I'll let Clem answer that," Malene said.

What was I supposed to say? But with all gazes on me, I took a small sip of sweet tea and replied, "To be honest, there have been times when the humans were frustrated with us. There was almost an uprising, even. A couple of men rode through town smearing us, but in the end we wound up becoming friends."

"Friends?" she asked, sounding surprised.

"Yeah." I smiled. "Even though we're different, we can still respect one another. The witches and wizards in our town don't abuse their powers. We don't hurt humans or attempt to control them in any way. There are lines that the magical beings in our town don't cross."

"Well said," Malene affirmed.

"Well," Trina replied with a smile, "and here I thought that I'd wind up fighting with humans. It's good to know that everyone gets along."

"Yes, we do," I added, omitting the fact that only a few weeks ago the clearers had been killing us off.

"It's the wizards you have to watch out for," Norma Ray said.

Trina dabbed her napkin to the corners of her mouth. "What do you mean?"

"They're the ones who might try to kill us, or even turn the humans against us."

The room went silent except for Norma Ray, who said, "Ouch! Malene, why'd you kick me?"

"I didn't kick you." Malene laughed nervously in Trina's direction. "She's mistaken."

But Norma Ray wouldn't shut it. "You kicked me because I said we've got to watch out for evil wizards. Well, one's coming to turn the humans against us. What's wrong with telling Trina that?"

I nearly smacked my face in frustration. *Everything's wrong with that, Norma Ray. Absolutely everything.*

CHAPTER 4

"And then Norma Ray let the cat out of the bag about the clearers," I told Rufus and Lady a little while later.

Rufus had come over for a slice of chocolate pie that Malene had made for me. Lady nibbled on a peanut butter treat that I'd bought for her.

"Oh, Norma Ray," Rufus said. "Leave it to her to spill the beans."

"She nearly told Trina everything. If she is the clearer, then she may suspect that we *suspect* her of being one." I cut a slice of pie for myself, plated it and dropped into a chair across the table from Rufus. "We managed to bandage the situation, but there's no telling what she thinks of us."

He finished chewing his bite and smiled. "I'm sure she thinks all of you are witches, and that Norma Ray is a few bananas short of a bunch."

I laughed. "Is that a saying?"

"It is now."

"I like it." We stared at each other for a long moment, so long that heat burned on my cheeks. "How's the pie?"

He dragged his gaze from mine back to the plate. "Amazing. I could eat this every day."

"In bed?" Lady asked.

I choked on the sip of coffee that I'd just taken. "What?"

"You know, you add the words 'in bed' to the end of sentences, like how you do when you read a fortune cookie." My dog cleared her throat and pretended to read a fortune. "You will have great luck this week. And then you add, 'in bed' to the end." I stared at her blankly. "Don't you know nothing about that, Clem?"

"Yes, but why are you bringing it up?" *When I could really grab Rufus by the shirt collar and drag him into my room?* "It's not appropriate conversation."

"Well, it must be, because people say 'in bed.' I saw that on YouTube."

I rolled my eyes. "I really need to start unplugging the television when I leave the house."

"I'd still find a way to watch it," she told me.

"Anyway," Rufus murmured, reining the conversation back in, "do you have plans to meet with Trina again?"

"No, I don't. But don't you think when the clearer arrives, they'll make a big show somehow?"

"Perhaps. Perhaps not." His brows tightened and he got a dark look on his face. "To sway people, you must first get them to warm to you. And second, you must have a cause."

"So you think the plan is to move slowly?"

"Hard to say. But from the clouds that rolled in the other day, I have no doubt that the clearer is here, doing the work of turning this town against us."

It was hard to just sit and not know who to battle. I wanted to jump up and start fighting, to end this before it even began, but without knowing who the enemy was, that was impossible.

Just as I was about to express my frustration, the doorbell rang. I answered it to find Jack standing on the other side of the screen door, awkwardly holding his staff and glancing over his shoulder every second.

"Jack, come in."

He stared up at the door and shook his head. "No, thank you. Ever since I've been living on the streets, I have a hard time going inside of places. They make me feel claustrophobic."

"Oh, okay."

Rufus was at my side. "What's going on? Have you learned something?"

"There's a new store in town, one I think it would be worth it for y'all to investigate."

Rufus and I exchanged a quick look. "I'll grab my purse."

I did so and Lady said, "Aren't you gonna take me? I'm perfect cover. No one will suspect that you're on the hunt with me in tow. And if they do, I'll bite their ankles until they bleed."

"Okay, I don't think there's any reason for you to resort to violence."

"Who said anything about violence? It ain't like I'm gonna kill nobody."

I scooped her into my arms. "Let's just keep things that way, all right?"

"Sounds good to me."

I locked up the house, and when we were all on the porch, Rufus said, "We're going downtown. There's a new weapons store that's opened up."

I frowned. "Weapons? Like magical weapons?"

"Nah," Jack said. "It's more like a bait and tackle shop with some knives and stuff."

And that was who was supposed to be our clearer? It didn't sound like it, but I was willing to investigate anything once.

"Well, what are we waiting for?" I said. "Let's go buy some bait."

WE STOOD outside the sporting goods shop that was smack in the middle of Main Street. The placard showed two shotguns crossed into an X, and above that it read *Guthrie's*. Signs in the windows advertised a grand opening.

"Did you know this was coming?" I asked Rufus.

He shook his head. "No idea." Then a wry smile lit up on his face. "Let's see exactly what Guthrie's is selling."

I'd been in a couple of sporting goods stores, but this one, for how small it was, was impressive.

The entire back wall was lined with rifles and shotguns. Workers helped a trove of men, bringing down weapons and presenting them. The rifles had glossy wooden stocks that shone under the display lights.

Now usually the knives were in back with the guns, displayed in a glass case. But here, the knives were separate, taking up an entire wall. There were all kinds of blades hanging—long swords and short swords. There were also maces and long daggers that looked slim enough to be hidden in a boot.

"Whoo wee," Jack said, whistling low, "looks like we've got quite a bit going on here."

"Can I help you?" asked a bald man behind the knife case.

"We came in to check out your new store," Rufus said.

The man extended his hand. "I'm Jody Guthrie and this is my place. Welcome."

"Good to be here," Rufus said.

Jack rubbed his cheek. "You sure do have a lot of steel behind you."

Jody chuckled. "Blades are my pride and joy. Don't get me wrong, I admire a well-made shotgun, too. But to me, the real artistry is in metalwork." He drummed his fingers on the glass. "Is there one I can show you?"

"How about that one there?" Jack told him, pointing to a really long samurai-looking blade.

"Absolutely." Jody pulled it down and settled it atop his fingers. "See the steelwork? There aren't any nicks, nor is there any discoloration in the blade. It's a perfect specimen of what bladesmithing truly is."

I peered over Jack's shoulder and saw what Jody meant. It was a beautiful blade.

Lady pawed at my legs. She wanted to see, too, so I lifted her to get a better look. She nodded her satisfaction, and I placed her back on the ground.

"You must've had to work overtime to get all these weapons in here so fast," Rufus said. "I don't remember seeing a sign that you'd be opening business soon."

Jody gave that friendly chuckle again. "To be honest, everything happened at once. We were looking for a new space. This one opened, and that was that. We moved in over the weekend and now we're here."

"Over the weekend," I murmured. "That's awfully fast. Why the rush?"

"We wanted to hit the ground running," Jody admitted. "That's how I've always done things."

"This steel," Jack murmured, "there's something in it."

Jody winked. "You found that, did you? Yes, all the steel has a little something special."

"What does that mean?" Rufus asked, his voice thick with suspicion.

"It means there's a touch of extra."

"Magic," I murmured.

Jody gave a slight nod. "Only those with power can sense it. Regular folks won't ever know about it. Oh, they'll realize the blade that they own is special, but they won't know why, and they won't be able to access the magic or do anything with it."

"What *can* we do with it?" I asked.

Jody smiled. "See for yourself."

He handed me a dagger as Jack was still preoccupied with the sword. The instant my fingers brushed the steel, a shock wave moved up my arm. I wrapped my fingers around the hilt and felt the power. This blade would go wherever I sent it. It would never miss a mark. It would pierce any bull's-eye that I aimed it at.

It was definitely attuned to my magic, and I was attuned to it as well.

"I like it," Jack said.

Jody smiled and I noticed a gold tooth in the back of his mouth peeking out. "Want to buy it?"

"Nah." He handed the sword to Jody, who ran a cloth over it before placing it back on the wall.

"How's that?" Rufus asked me.

Honestly it was hard to tear myself away from the blade, but I wasn't about to purchase a dagger. "See for yourself."

He took the blade and his eyes widened. "Very powerful indeed." To Jody he said, "What sort of magic is that?"

Jody did that whole winking thing again. "The sort that's been in my family for generations. Family secret, we like to say."

Family secret. *Shmumily* secret. We were all witches, and most witches shared that sort of stuff.

"You have to understand," he explained. "This is my business. Me telling you would be like Coca-Cola revealing their recipe. It's not going to happen."

But perhaps it should have.

Rufus smiled tightly. "I understand. You have a business to run and a profit to make."

"Exactly." He laughed, "And if I told you, I'd have to kill you."

There was a pause before we all chuckled. Oh, death jokes were just way too hilarious.

Not at all.

Jody placed the dagger back up on the wall. "Well, you know where to come if you're ever looking for protection. These knives will do you good if something bad happens. In this day and age," he said pointedly, "you can never be too careful. Y'all have heard about what's going on with our kind, haven't you?"

"We have," I murmured.

He nodded. "Then you know that your own magic may not be the best protection for you. You could wind up needing something else, something like this. You never know, a dagger such as this might save your life."

"Maybe another time," I said.

We thanked him and were about to leave when voices shouted from the other side of the shop, the gun side.

A customer pointed a shotgun at another customer. The man had flung hands up in fear.

The man pointing the gun said, "You come one step closer, and I'll blow your head off!"

CHAPTER 5

Rufus rushed into the melee, palm up, ready to throw magic. "Put the gun down."

The gunman, who wore a red baseball cap with a sweat stain around the rim, said over his shoulder, never taking his gaze off the man he had the gun trained on, "This guy here, he was trying to take this shotgun from me. He wanted it, and he wanted it bad."

"It's not even yours," the other man spat. He wore a pair of camo fatigues as if he was one of those weekend warrior types. His tight black shirt tore at his cut biceps, and his hair was shaved to within an inch of his scalp.

Course, he might not have been a weekend warrior. He could have actually been military, I realized.

"What's your name?" Rufus asked the gunshot-toting man.

"Roy."

"Roy, why don't we talk about this as civilized people? Without pointing weapons at one another."

"No," Roy said.

Rufus and Jody exchanged a look. Jody had a dagger on his hip and he pointed to it, but Rufus shook his head.

"What's your name?" Rufus asked the would-be victim.

"Stanley," he answered.

"Tell me what happened."

"Well, I was minding my own business. This man here, Roy, he was looking at shotguns. He'd had this one pulled down, but he'd set it aside. So I picked it up. That was when he yanked it from my hands, loaded it and pointed it at me."

The man behind the counter nodded, corroborating Stanley's story.

To Roy, Rufus said, "It sounds like Stanley thought that you were finished seeing the weapon. I don't think he meant any harm."

"Don't matter what he meant," Roy spat. "It's what he did that counts."

The whole while, Roy kept that gun trained on Stanley's head. Some people had fled the building, but others were hanging around. I'm sure someone was videoing the scene with the help of their phone.

There are always folks who taped situations where someone attacks another in public. They didn't get involved; they just watched innocent people being harmed and then shared it for all the world to see.

Those upstanding citizens (heavy sarcasm here).

"Roy," Rufus said, "you can see the gun and hold it without pointing it at anyone. Now. Why don't you just put it down?"

"I'm calling the police," Jody said.

"Don't you dare!" Roy swiveled the gun toward him, and those who remained in the store gasped. "You call anybody and I'll shoot you dead."

Rufus's back was to me, but I saw his shoulders tense. Instead of anyone de-escalating the situation, Jody had just intensified it.

"No one's going to call the police," Rufus tried to assure him.

"That ain't what he just said," Roy shouted. "He's gonna call the cops and get me arrested."

"Listen," Rufus replied in a soothing voice, "we all just want to be friends here. All of us. No one wants to harm anyone. Now, please. Put the gun away. Calm down. Let's all take a deep breath. Besides, what do you want to happen, Roy? Do you actually want to shoot someone?"

"I don't want nobody touching my gun!"

I had a feeling that Roy was dealing with deep psychological issues, the type that would be best handled by authorities.

"And if anyone here even thinks about leaving this shop, you're gonna be shot first," he warned.

I knew that Rufus had just about had it at that point. He would have to take rash measures, and quickly.

"Roy, hand me the gun."

"No."

"Then you leave me no choice."

Rufus took a step toward Roy, and Roy pointed the end of the shotgun at him. "Don't come any closer, or I swear that I'll shoot."

Stanley, feeling either very brave or very stupid, lunged for the gun. He reached for the weapon, his finger wrapping over Roy's trigger hand.

That was when the barrel exploded.

It was aimed right at Rufus's chest.

Smoke and fire shot from the end. In less than a second, a ball of light flared from Rufus's palm. It enveloped Roy and Stanley, lifting them both up into the air and dropping them like lead weights to the floor.

They were knocked unconscious. I darted to Rufus, coming around to witness the damage.

There was a hole the size of a quarter in his shoulder. I reached for him as Rufus grimaced. He then took an orb from his pocket and pressed it to the wound. A yellow light glowed in the hole, and when it faded several seconds later, the wound was healed.

"Did you get that?" someone shouted.

"Oh, man! I'm uploading that to TikTok right now!"

"I'm putting it on Twitter," another person shouted.

"Did you see that? Instagram is gonna crash!"

Rufus pulled me into a hug, and I realized that in that moment our lives would never be the same again. The entire world was about to see what Rufus had done. I only prayed that instead of our kind becoming the villains, Rufus was hailed as a hero.

But I had my doubts that would happen.

"You okay?" Jody asked, clasping Rufus's shoulder.

Rufus pulled away from our hug and said, "We shall soon see."

I agreed. We would soon see indeed.

THE POLICE HAULED Roy away without many questions after they saw the video that had already gone viral before Tuney Sluggs even arrived on the scene. Once he was shown the footage, he simply asked what had led up to the situation, nodded at Rufus and told him that he could leave.

Jody was more verbal, telling Rufus he could have any blade on display that he wanted. You know, for saving people's lives and all.

Rufus demurely declined, though Jody insisted.

From the way his brows were stitched together, it was obvious that all Rufus wanted to do was go to his house and decompress.

Finally, after what felt like five hours, we left.

"You okay?" Jack asked when we were outside the shop.

Rufus forced a smile. "For the moment I am. But what the future holds, I don't know."

Jack rubbed a hand over his whiskers. "I'll keep an ear out, try to discover what folks are saying."

I already knew what would drip from their wagging tongues. I could just hear the gossips. *Rufus Mayes nearly killed a man with magic. We'd all better be careful or else we'll be his next victims.*

Rufus thanked Jack and we left. "I can drop you off at your house," I told him.

"That's fine."

I expected Lady to make a comment about seeing Rufus's home, but she was oddly silent. Even she sensed the heaviness of the day.

When we reached his house, I offered to make Rufus some tea. "That would be nice," he told me.

I set about finding the tea and making him a cup. All the tea he had was black and full of caffeine. What he needed was something relaxing. It took a while to find it, but I eventually located a box of Sleepytime in the very back of his cupboard.

"Bingo."

I made the tea and took it into his living room. Rufus had the news on and was watching. "Trying to see if anyone's talking about this yet."

I placed the cup on the table in front of him. "Maybe we'll get lucky and it won't be on the airwaves."

He shot me a skeptical look. "You saw how people were uploading it." He grimaced. "I should have erased the videos, but I didn't think about it. What a stupid mistake to have made."

"It's not your fault." I pressed a hand to his shoulder. "Look. You were a bit busy today, saving people's lives. Go easy on yourself. It's not your fault that you didn't think about that. I didn't, either."

Not that I would've known how to erase a video off someone's phone. But I might've figured out how to make the phone explode or something. That was about how effective I was with magic.

But I was worried, too. A scene like what had happened today, if it got out into the big, wide world, could either help our situation and make Rufus a hero, or it could make him an enemy of the people.

"And breaking today," said the newscaster, "is this video that just went viral. We received it moments ago, and it apparently shows a man using what some are calling magic."

My heart pounded so hard I thought it might pop out of my chest. The clip cut away from the woman at the news desk and up flashed the video. Another reporter was doing a voice-over for the story.

"Today, a man in the town of Peachwood, Alabama, used what appeared to be magic in order to stop a man who was threatening the lives of others in a local sporting goods store."

As the reporter spoke, I saw Roy point his shotgun at Rufus and fire. Then Rufus fired magic at him, causing Roy to fall back, tumbling to the ground.

The video stopped and up came the picture of a man reporting from in front of Guthrie's. His hair was cropped short, and his dark skin shone under the camera lights.

"Behind me is the store where it all happened. Some are calling this local man a hero, while others aren't so sure."

Up came a montage of locals speaking into a microphone. The first I instantly recognized as Dooley Hutto, whom I'd done some work for.

He would definitely be on Rufus's side.

"Well, I don't know about no magic," Dooley said, "but I can tell you if some crazy man threw some light-looking stuff like that at me, we'd have had a tussle."

I rolled my eyes. Dooley was seventy years old. He wasn't about to tussle with anybody physically. Oh, he could throw some good old-fashioned word punches, but that was about the extent of it.

The clip cut to Claire, who Malene had argued with at church. Claire smiled politely to the reporter. *"Peachwood's had a long history of magic. We all know about it. But the fact is, those magic people stay on their side of town and leave the rest of us alone. At least, that's how it's always been. But if they start attacking us humans...well, I think something will have to be done about them."*

I squeezed Rufus's shoulder, and he gloved my hand, squeezing it back. I sensed that we were both thinking the same thing—that this was bad. So far, no one had stood up for anyone with magic. But maybe the reporter would find someone, anyone who was on our side.

The last person to talk was Georgie, a man we knew held magical abilities. He was also tied to the wizard mafia that existed in Peachwood. If anyone would be on our side, it would be Georgie.

"Well, there's a time and a place for magic," he explained to the camera, *"and using it to scare people is never good."*

"Did the magic scare you?" the reporter asked.

"Oh yes. I've been scared of magic lots of times in my life."

"What?" I nearly shouted. "What was he talking about? He's a wizard and he wasn't even in the store when it happened!"

The report cut back to the newscaster live downtown. *"And there you have it, Natasha. That's what the folks of this sleepy town are saying about what happened today. Some are frightened and some simply don't know what to do."*

The live feed returned to the studio where the female newscaster sat behind the desk. *"An interesting story, Niles. Be sure to keep us updated on any breaking events. And that's all for the evening news. Thank you for watching."*

As the tape rolled to the credits, I slowly turned to Rufus. I didn't know what to say, and his expression was grim.

It was Lady who spoke. "Well, y'all, it looks like we're screwed."

I had a feeling that she was right.

CHAPTER 6

"Wat the heck happened today?" Malene said when I answered the phone.

I'd left Rufus after the newscast. He didn't have much to say. It seemed like he needed to think about next moves, and as I was at a complete loss with nothing to contribute, I just went on home.

Soon as I stepped inside the door, Malene was ringing my phone off the hook—my landline, not the cell.

"Well? Aren't you going to answer me?" Malene asked when it took me a moment to collect my thoughts. "Rufus just attacked someone?"

"No. What? He didn't attack anyone."

"That's not what the news is reporting."

"Well, they're wrong. We went to the new sporting goods store—a place, by the way that opened suspiciously quickly—and while there, someone loaded a shotgun and threatened to hurt another customer. The man shot at Rufus, and the rest is history."

"Well, it's on Wolf News, too."

I exhaled. "The conservative channel?"

"Yep, and they're asking if Rufus used his magic in the right way. Everyone is wondering that."

"Just five minutes ago the story was only local."

"Well, it's gone national, chicken," Malene snapped. "It must be a slow news day, because the entire country's talking about it."

I filled Lady's bowl with food and flipped on the television. Every channel I turned to was showing the same video, and all the talking heads, panels of them, were discussing if it was right for Rufus to have used magic. Half of the people didn't even think that what they saw was magic, while the other half was proclaiming that magic had always been around, it had simply been kept secret. Except for evil Rufus, who had used it on a poor gun-wielding terrorist.

That's how folks were treating this. Half of them supported Rufus, and the other half were calling his actions threatening. They said that if wizards couldn't be controlled, then they needed to be locked away, their magic stripped from them somehow.

My heart sank as I soaked up the story.

"Clem? You there?" Malene said.

I'd forgotten that I was still holding the phone. I brought it to my ear. "Yeah, I'm here."

"The one thing we wanted to be, calm and cool, is now gone. This story gives the clearers exactly what they want—to blame magic for being evil and turn the town against us."

"I know that. But Rufus had to do it."

"I understand," she told me. "But we've got to come up with a plan B. By this time tomorrow the entire town's going to know what happened."

"The town? I'm more worried about the world."

"Don't be. The twenty-four-hour news cycle will quickly forget about Rufus and what happened. The government might not, though."

"What?" I said, panicking. "The government?"

"Don't freak out just yet," Malene told me. "We need to take one problem at a time. First, we need to spin this story our way."

What was she talking about, spin the story? "I'm not following."

"We need a photo op with Rufus playing with a litter of puppies or something, something that makes him look gentle, not frightening at all. That should alleviate some of the tension in town. If we can do it right, that is."

I started to argue and stopped. Malene might have been crazy, but I didn't think she was wrong. In order to squash any negative thoughts about Rufus, we did need to get ahead of the story. We had to create our own press, something positive.

"Malene, you're a genius."

"Thank you," she said with a triumphant sniff. "It's always good when my brilliance is recognized."

"Um, yes. Now we've just got to figure out the best way to go about things."

She started to come up with her plan, and I grabbed a pen and paper. "Yes," I murmured. "That sounds good. Absolutely. Sure, I can do that."

Within ten minutes we'd hatched a solid idea, one that would hopefully get any potential negative media or emotions off our backs.

We'd meet this challenge head-on and convince the troubled people of Peachwood that Rufus was not in any way going to harm them. That he'd only been acting in self-defense and they didn't need to worry about him.

We hung up the phone and I cheered. Lady looked up at me from her food bowl, kibble dropping from her mouth to the floor.

"Everything all right?" she questioned.

"Yes. Everything is great." I grabbed my cell and thumbed it to life. "I just need to convince Rufus to do a photo op, and we should be golden." He answered on the second ring. "Listen, Malene and I have a great idea, one that will salvage this whole fiasco."

"Oh good, I hope so," he said in a low voice, almost a growl.

Him being upset was understandable. But I wasn't going to let his bad mood spoil the plan. "Can we meet tomorrow?"

"Maybe."

"What? Why maybe?"

"That's if I can get out of my house in the morning."

I frowned. "Why wouldn't you be able to?"

"Because my street is currently crawling with reporters, and their cameras are aimed at my front door."

Oh crap. The media attack of Rufus Mayes had already begun. What could go wrong next?

∼

BUT HE WAS able to meet downtown in the morning. "I had to use magic to slip out unseen," he told me when we paired up at Bender's.

"You're kidding."

He pulled his dark sunglasses down so that I could see his eyes. "Do I look like I'm joking?"

No, he didn't. "Ugh. I figured the reporters would have been gone by now."

"So did I."

"Good morning," Julie said in greeting. "Rufus, are you trying to be incognito?"

I answered for him. "Yes, thanks to a certain situation that happened yesterday."

She frowned. "I heard that Rufus is a hero."

"Well, apparently heroes and villains are cut from the same cloth," he said.

"I'm sorry about that," she said. "Listen, why don't you get one of Trina's special lattes? It'll make you feel better after one sip."

"I'd rather an espress—"

"He'll take a latte," I said quickly. "And I'll have my usual."

After he paid and we stepped away from the counter, Rufus said, "Would you like to explain why I can't have my espresso?"

"Because Trina's new here and we're doing her a favor."

"I would have liked a favor by having my favorite drink."

"You'll like the latte."

He didn't look convinced. But we headed over to the end of the counter and waited. Trina spotted me and smiled.

"Hey, Clem, how're you?"

"Doing great. How's Bender's treating you?"

Trina wiped down the steam arm with a cloth. "I can't complain. Julie says business has picked up immensely since I started."

"Wow. Cool."

"Cinnamon latte," Trina announced.

A woman brushed past us and took the cup from the counter. "I hope this is as good as I've heard."

Trina smiled widely. "It will be."

The woman took a tentative sip and sighed. "My dear, this is heaven in a cup. Thank you. Thank you very much!"

She dropped a dollar in the tip jar and scurried away.

"Well, looks like you're doing something right."

Trina giggled. "I sure do hope so. Now. Let me make y'all's drinks."

She whipped up Rufus's latte and my chocolate mocha in no time. Rufus took a sip and smiled. "Thank you. It's very good."

So was my mocha. It was like drinking a river made of chocolate and coffee. I could've gone sailing down it, it was so amazing. "Yum. This is delicious."

As we headed out, I noticed that the people in the coffee shop were all smiling. All of them. That was unusual. Usually folks were consumed with their own business—reading the paper, texting their friends. But not today. Today, people were mingling with one another.

That was odd. Was there some event going on that I had missed?

Before I had the chance to ask Julie, my phone rang. Malene's name lit up the screen. "Good morning!"

"Where're you at?" she demanded.

"Just grabbing some coffee. We're on our way."

"Well, hurry up. These puppies are wiggly, and besides, the news crews should be here any minute. I don't want them leaving because y'all aren't here."

"Don't worry, we'll be there." I covered the mouthpiece and said to Rufus, "It's Malene."

"Tell her we'll arrive in less than five minutes."

"It'll be five minutes," I repeated into the phone.

"It better be. Now hurry up."

I hung up and slipped the phone into my purse. "What's stuck in her craw?"

He smirked. "I suppose it's a bunch of puppies."

"What gives you that idea?"

Rufus pointed down the road. "Look."

Sure enough, sitting on the sidewalk were Malene, Urleen, Norma Ray and what looked like a small mountain of puppies.

"What in the world?" I said. "I thought that this was going to be only a few puppies. Just enough to show that you're a kind person."

"Apparently a few to you and a few to Malene are different things."

Malene saw us and stepped forward, only she couldn't get very far because ten puppies attacked her leg.

Norma Ray spotted us and threw her hands up. "Rufus, thank goodness that you're here. There are so many puppies. They're crawling all over me."

She paused and stuck her hand down the front of her blouse. When she pulled it back out, she held a puppy. "It's like those videos of farms in Australia overrun by bunnies. Have you ever seen all the bunnies they have in Australia? They're natural pests."

"No, I'm sorry to say that I haven't," he told her.

All I could do was stand and stare in disbelief. There must have been, and I'm not exaggerating, at least fifty puppies crawling all over the small bales of hay that had been set up like a chair on the sidewalk.

"Where did all of them come from?" I asked.

Urleen pulled apart two furry brown puppies that were fighting over her shoe. "I've got a niece who breeds dogs. Turns out, she had a bumper litter."

"More like ten bumper litters," I replied, astounded.

Malene jumped into action. "Okay, Rufus. You're going to sit here." She steered him to the rudimentary seat made from bales. "All you have to do is sit here for just a minute, and the paparazzi—I mean journalists —should arrive."

"And what's the story?" he asked. "Am I being attacked by puppies?"

"No, of course not," Norma Ray said with a laugh. "You're rescuing them."

"From what?" I asked.

"From that."

She pointed, along with Malene and Urleen at a crude sign made from dirty one by six boards that had been sloppily covered with white paint. On it, in red letters that dripped (because the paint wasn't completely dry) were the words, *PUPPY SOUP FOR SALE!*

Rufus blinked. "I'm sorry?"

"You saved the puppies from being turned into puppy soup," Malene explained. "Isn't it obvious?"

"But who was going to turn puppies into soup?" I asked, pointing out the hole in her devilish plot.

"The same people who do evil things," Norma Ray explained.

Malene and Urleen nodded in satisfaction. "Exactly," Malene said. A news van pulled up and parked on the street. Malene pushed Rufus onto the hay bales. "Okay, it's showtime. Make this look good."

39

CHAPTER 7

Within minutes there were five camera crews all with their lenses trained on Rufus. He sat on the bales while puppies nipped at his clothing and one jumped on his head.

There were so many of them that they reminded me of rodents more than they did dogs. It was unsettling. I wasn't sure that I'd ever be the same after watching them swarm all over Rufus.

I was also certain he would have to burn the clothes that he was wearing when the whole thing was done, too.

"Rufus Mayes, I understand that you were the man who used magic against that gunman yesterday at the sporting goods store, Guthrie's," a female reporter wearing a suit and skirt said. "Would you like to comment on that? Were you out of line to use magic? Was it even magic that you used or some trick?"

"Some reports say that you caused the shotgun to fire," a blond man said, shoving the microphone into Rufus's face. "What do you have to say about that?"

"We're here today," Malene said with authority, "because this man just saved these puppies from becoming puppy soup."

The reporters all eyed Malene for a moment. Then the woman turned back to Rufus. "What do you say to your critics out there, the folks who think that you abused your ability to use magic?"

"That you shouldn't have used it in the way that you did," the man followed up.

"He has to say"—Malene stepped forward, standing right beside Rufus—"that he's here for the puppies. Now, can you please ask him about the puppies?"

"Is magic evil? Does it even exist?" the woman pushed.

"Do you regret what happened yesterday?" the other reporter asked. "From what I hear, Roy Clayvin was knocked out for a full hour after you attacked him."

"The puppies," Malene shouted.

No one paid attention to her. At that point, severely frustrated, she made a face at Norma Ray, who nodded and slipped unnoticed down the street.

Finally Rufus spoke, and I could practically see the saliva rolling off the reporter's tongues. In their minds, they were getting next-to-exclusive coverage.

"What happened yesterday occurred because one man threatened to harm others. I was there and my goal was to make sure that didn't happen, and I would say that I was successful."

"But what about your naysayers, those who think you acted too harshly?" the woman asked. "People believe that magic shouldn't be used to harm others."

"Neither should any weapon," Rufus retorted. "But that was what would have happened if I hadn't stepped in."

"But was using magic the right call?" the man asked. "When you could have called the police and let them handle it?"

Now there were several other reporters on the sidewalk, all with cameras or phones aimed at Rufus, soaking up his every word.

"Let the police handle it?" Rufus asked with disgust, repeating the reporter's question. "When that man had his shotgun aimed at another man and was inches from pulling the trigger? Right. You didn't see that part, did you? All you, the media, saw was the part when I used magic. Did any of you bother to watch what led up to that moment? You think that perhaps I simply started wielding magic and Roy aimed the shotgun on me to get me to stop, is that it?"

"That has been theorized," the woman admitted.

"That is the farthest thing from the truth." A vein in Rufus's forehead popped. He was ticked now. This didn't look good for Malene's photo op. "The truth was that Roy Clayvin was unstable. He thought another man was going to take that shotgun away from him, so he loaded it and aimed it at him. He started the altercation. I intervened to save a life. Roy aimed the gun at me because I was attempting to save a man. Then he fired and I fired back, but with magic. I'm sorry if that doesn't fit your narrative. Now, you have my words on camera and can edit them however you see fit. Don't. Let my story stand as the truth."

There were no questions for half a minute, which was when Malene took the opportunity to shout, "But the puppies!" No one paid any attention until she shouted even louder, "Look! The soup bandit is attempting to steal them! Get him, Rufus!"

Everyone glanced to where she was pointing, and I nearly burst out laughing. There, dressed in a black pantsuit with a cape, stood Norma Ray. For a disguise she had placed a black bandana with eyeholes over her face. The best way to describe how she looked was that all she needed was a big floppy hat and she and the Hamburglar could've been twins.

"Someone stop him. Er, I mean her," Malene shouted.

Norma Ray scooped up about fifteen puppies and put them into a basket. "Now, I'm going to cook and eat these puppies! I'm going to make my favorite stew." She cackled like the Wicked Witch of the West and started to walk quickly down the street. "You'll never catch me!"

Really. How far had we stooped? How had I let Malene talk me into this? Yesterday this had seemed like a decent idea. But that was before the whole "puppy soup" thing had been invented.

Malene shook Rufus. "Stop her. You've got to stop her with your magic. Do it!"

"Yes," the female reporter said, "do it! Save the puppies!"

Was she for real?

"Let's see you work some real magic," the male reporter added.

Why were they cheering him on? Then I understood. They each wanted to be the reporter to break the story, to have an eyewitness account of Rufus working magic.

I didn't like it one bit. "Don't do it," I told Rufus.

Rufus pulled a sea of puppies off his lap and rose. "Listen, this has all been a great idea, but I don't think—"

"Stop her," Malene shouted, taking Rufus by the arm. She aimed him in the direction of Norma Ray the Hamburgler. "Use your magic for good! Prove to these people that you only have good intentions with your power."

So at that point, not only was the press here, but there was also a crowd of people who had appeared. It was early. Where had they come from? There were so many of them it was like they were seeping from the woodwork, or better yet, the cracks in the cement.

Malene had not released her hold on Rufus, though. She was hanging on tight, one hand clamped over his. "Shoot that bandit!"

"Malene," Rufus said apologetically. "This has all been a mistake. I don't need to prove anything."

Didn't he, though? The way that the media had framed some of their questions, it was obvious that they weren't painting Rufus as the hero. They wanted a villain, and they wanted him to be magical.

That fit their narrative.

Rufus tried to pull away from Malene's grasp, but she wouldn't let him. "No! Stop her!"

"Look," Norma Ray called. "I'm getting away with the puppies. You know what I'm going to do with them!"

I looked at Urleen. "Did this really seem like a good idea?"

She shrugged. "To Malene it did. Of course, anything that involves puppies seems like a good idea to her."

"But eating them?"

"Puts them in danger," she explained with a nod of her head. "That's what the kids want nowadays—excitement. And what's more exciting than a puppy snatcher?"

She had me there.

Malene was pulling Rufus, who I knew didn't want to make any sudden moves that could hurt my grandmother. "Come on! Get her! She's going to eat those puppies!"

"Let's just settle down," Rufus said.

That was when Malene somehow got magic to shoot from Rufus's hand. Don't ask me how she did it, but the next thing I knew, a ball of power was zipping toward Norma Ray, who was facing the opposite direction. She didn't see it coming toward her.

"Norma—I mean, Puppy Snatcher," Malene called. "Look out!"

Norma Ray waddled around and spied the magic. She bent down to avoid being hit, and the magic crashed into one of the beams holding up the awning that ran down Main Street.

"Get out," I called. "Everybody go!"

Rufus acted quick as lightning. He scooped up all the puppies in a bubble of magic and whisked them onto the street. Then he grabbed Malene and rushed toward Norma Ray.

Meanwhile I shooed the reporters out.

"The awning's gonna fall," the woman cried.

"Get out of my way," the man yelled. "I'm too beautiful to die!"

The awning groaned and shook as if we were experiencing an earthquake. I had just gotten on the street along with everyone else (and the mountain of puppies), when I turned to watch the inevitable avalanche.

The awning was swaying and was about to crash to the ground when Rufus, in a very superhero way, pointed to one side of it and magic unfurled from his fingers. The post holding the structure collapsed and the steel awning started to fall, but the magic reached it before it could crumble.

The awning hovered in the air a moment before Rufus aimed another line of magic at it. Then, very slowly, and with a lot of groaning, the steel structure slowly lifted and was put back into place. Rufus repaired the column and fixed the entire structure as we watched.

Those in attendance, even the Hamburgler, cheered for him.

Rufus smiled shyly. "Thank you. It was nothing."

All the while, the cameras were rolling.

"Rufus," the woman asked, running up to him with the microphone in hand, "how does it feel to be a hero?"

Oh, so now he was a hero? What a quick change of heart the media had.

"Well, that was nothing, really," he said. "I'm not a hero."

"But you just saved the town's structure," the man said. "You are a hero."

Rufus shook his head. "I thank all of you for coming, but I must be going."

He started to walk off, but the reporters were at his heels. At the same time I spotted the puppies. They'd been left in the middle of the street. Malene had forgotten about them in all the drama of the awning.

A sportscar turned a corner, heading down Main. The driver was looking down at his phone and didn't look up, which meant that he didn't see the puppies sitting smack-dab in the middle of the street.

"The puppies," I shouted.

Everyone turned at once. And everyone, at once, realized what was about to happen.

Rufus raised his hand as the driver looked up. Seeing the puppies, he jerked the steering wheel to the left and veered straight into a fire hydrant.

Water geysered from the hydrant, shooting straight up into the air and out the sides.

We all stood shocked at the scene. The car's driver got out and looked at the puppies. "Who left all those puppies in the middle of the road?"

He sounded none too pleased that he'd wrecked his car to avoid hitting them.

Very slowly, all gazes turned to Rufus.

"He did it," Malene accused.

"It was him," the Hamburgler seconded.

Then all the wonder, all the cheering that had gone Rufus's way stopped. You could even see the expressions on the reporter's faces change in that split second. One moment they were on his side, and the next, they were against him.

The male reporter thrust out his microphone. "Would you like to explain to us why you left puppies in the middle of the road?"

"Yes," the woman asked, "did you do it so that they would be killed, just like you hoped would happen to Roy in the sporting goods store?"

Malene slapped her face. I wanted to as well.

Any hope that Rufus would be redeemed by the media had gone up in smoke. Now he would be painted as the devil, and all because of a few dozen puppies.

CHAPTER 8

$\mathcal{I}$ didn't bother watching the news. What was the point? It was obvious how the media would spin what had happened that morning.

All the good stuff about Rufus would be edited out—him saving the awning, sitting with a lapful of puppies. It would be replaced with him abandoning puppies to die in the middle of the road.

That would be the story that the media went with.

Anyway, after the entire fiasco downtown, Rufus headed home and so did I. I think that we knew there wasn't anything that could be done to salvage the situation, at least not at that point.

My phone rang while I was at home. I saw Malene's name flare on the screen and ignored it. I had no intention of talking to her—at least not for several weeks.

Oh, she'd apologized for everything that had happened. But my goodness, she'd been the person who caused the awning to fall in the first place. It had been her own magic that she'd shot at Norma Ray. On top of that, my grandmother had pointed the proverbial finger at Rufus and told the cameras that he had been the person who left the puppies in the road.

No, no. She didn't bother to mention that she'd been the one who rounded them up in the first place.

So the whole thing was an absolute mess, and I needed to decompress from my family. Well, from Malene.

"What's wrong, sugar?" Lady asked that afternoon. "You haven't gotten out of bed since you came home and got back into it."

I stared at my oversize T-shirt and the three empty teacups on my nightstand. "What? Can't a girl just lie in bed all day?"

"A girl can," she said from the floor, "but not you. That ain't like you. Where's your gusto? Your *joie de vivre*, as the Frenchies say?"

"Have you been watching the foreign film channel again?"

"I cain't tell a lie. Yes, I have been."

I laughed. "Well, my joy for life went out the window today. Everyone in town is going to think Rufus is a horrible wizard with no regard for human or puppy life."

"Aw, nobody's going to think that, Clem."

I shot her a pointed look. "I told you what happened when I got home."

"Okay, they *might* think those things about him. But we know the truth."

I sighed and fell back against a down pillow. "The truth isn't going to matter when the clearers show up and start converting people to their way of thinking. None of it will matter."

"Do you know what you need?" She sat and wagged her tail, letting it sweep across the rug. "You need to take me for a walk."

I sighed. "Is that the answer to all my problems?"

"It might not be the answer, but it sure as heck will relieve my bladder."

I threw off the covers and placed my bare feet on the soft rug. "Okay. I'm up. Let's go for a walk."

When I thought of walks, what came to mind was taking Lady around the block maybe once. But that day, she had another route planned.

"Let's walk downtown."

"That's far away. You'll never make it on those short legs of yours."

She shot me a contemptuous look. "That's why you're gonna drive us. Then we'll walk."

"Oh, okay. Let me get this straight—we're going to drive to where we're going for a walk."

"Yep. And if we pass that pizza food truck, can I have a slice?"

"Maybe. If you're good."

"I'll be good."

We headed off and arrived downtown a few minutes later. There was no telling how many folks had seen what occurred that morning, so I decided to steer clear of the main throng of people, instead focusing on side streets that were less busy.

"Why ain't we heading toward the pizza truck?" Lady asked.

"Was that your whole intention of coming here? To eat pizza?"

"And what if it was?"

"Well…I guess that I would say you're one smart dog for convincing me that all you actually wanted was to go for a walk."

"Got to burn off those calories somehow."

I smiled. "Come on. Let's get some exercise, and then we'll swing by the pizza truck."

The late afternoon air was cool. The sun was setting, and the bright colors streaked the sky. The humidity wasn't so terribly strong. In another month it would be horrible. But for the moment it had receded and a slight wind blew, caressing my neck and reminding me of why I loved evenings in the South.

The cicadas had come out and were buzzing, their song filling the air. It eased my weary heart and put a spring into my step.

We had reached the church, and I noticed that the parking lot was full, which was strange as it wasn't a sermon night. There also wasn't a sign on the billboard advertising any special service, so I hadn't missed the announcement that it was revival week or anything like that.

But still, I spotted Claire Rose getting out of her car and going inside. If Malene discovered that I'd seen Claire going into the church and I didn't relay the incident, then I'd be in the doghouse for weeks.

Not that I cared, but it was still a good idea to investigate. At least then I'd be armed with knowledge that my grandmother might or might not want.

I tugged Lady toward the church. "Where're we going? You feeling like confessing or something like that?"

I smirked. "We're Baptists. We don't confess. That's Catholics."

"Well, what are you doing taking me to church?"

"Cleansing your soul," I said sarcastically.

"My soul don't need cleansed. My soul's as clean as it's ever going to be. Don't nobody need to be worried about my soul."

I rolled my eyes. "I'm only joking. Come on. Let's see what's going on."

The door to the sanctuary creaked as I opened it. I winced, hoping that I hadn't disturbed anyone. When no one in the pews turned around, I released a breath and shuffled inside, sitting in the back.

Pastor Clark walked up onto the preaching stage. Pastor Steve was still sick?

He spoke. "I want to thank those of you who've come. In the short time that I've visited with y'all, I've seen that some of you have needs, some healing that must be done. Don't we all need healing? We talk so much about spiritual healing in the church, and we know that our bodies will, at some point, fail us. But if we can gain physical healing, then we should."

He looked down in the pews. "Claire, will you please come here?" She made her way up to him, and he took both of her hands in his. "When I met you the other day, what did I tell you?"

She hesitated. "That, um…"

"It's okay, you can tell them."

I'd picked up Lady and sat seated beside her. She whispered. "What in tarnation is going on?"

"I have no idea."

"Why's he talking to that woman?" she persisted.

"I don't know. But if you're quiet, I'm sure that we can find out."

Hurt, she replied, "I was only asking."

I patted her head. "I'm just saying."

From the pulpit, Pastor Clark repeated, "Claire? What did I tell you?"

She glanced to the floor for a moment. "Well, you said that God had a special plan for me, and that I should come here."

He looked out. "I told all of you to come here tonight. Because there's something special that I want to show you. Pastor Steve has told me wonderful things about all of you. He loves each of you, and I want to continue the blessing he's given you. Y'all have been so welcoming to me that I want to show you thanks. God wants to show his thanks."

A few people murmured, no doubt wondering how God was going

to show his thanks. It was the same thing that I was wondering. What was Pastor Clark talking about? Was he going to reward everyone with a new car or something?

Just kidding. I knew that there were no new cars involved.

But anyway, Lady yawned and snuggled up to me, closing her eyes as Pastor Clark continued. "May I see your hand?" Claire gave him her good one. "Not that one," he corrected.

Ever so slowly, she pulled her shriveled hand from her pocket. He took it gently and gloved it between his two. He stood there a moment, and Claire's gaze swiveled around the room as if she was looking for the nearest escape.

"This makes you uncomfortable, doesn't it?" he said.

She nodded. "Yes, it does."

He spoke to the congregation. "Why is it that our shortcomings, those things which make us unique, are what we shy away from? God has given us these differences, and we should take pride in that. We should weaponize these as battle scars in the army of righteousness."

"Amen," someone said.

Clark smiled kindly. "But I do understand why you don't want to advertise this. Because even though it is a gift from God, it makes you feel less whole, less like one of his children. Remember, we are all God's children. Every one of us. Don't forget that. Well now, Claire, with the power of God, I am going to make you feel whole. Close your eyes." She looked around again, unsure of just what exactly the pastor had in store for her. So he repeated again, "Close your eyes."

This time she did so, and he prayed. Everyone bowed their heads except for me, because I wanted to see what was going on. What was Pastor Clark talking about the healing of God?

He thanked God for our lives and for the blessings that he had bestowed. "And Lord," he said, "I ask that you show this woman your love. She has worn this battle scar a long time. Let her be healed so that we may all witness your glory. Amen."

When the congregation opened their eyes, Claire was the first one to gasp. Pastor Clark pulled his hands away, and she lifted her small, withered one.

Only it was withered no more.

She flexed the fingers and turned it this way and that before exclaiming, "I'm healed! Pastor Clark has healed me! Oh my goodness. It's a miracle. Glory be to God!"

She flung her arms around his neck, nearly knocking him over.

"It wasn't me, Claire. It was God. I'm only his vessel."

Claire raced down the steps, throwing her hand in the faces of the attendees. "Look, y'all! I'm healed. Everyone, I'm healed! God is great!"

A round of amens came from the pews while Pastor Clark looked on and smiled. When Claire sat, he said to the rest in attendance, "Now. Who would like to receive God's miracle next?"

Every hand in the sanctuary lifted except for mine. Lady stirred and smacked her lips. "What's going on?"

"Either a miracle," I answered, "or the devil pretending to be cloaked in God's goodness."

"Well, which is it?"

I shook my head. "I don't know, but I plan to find out."

CHAPTER 9

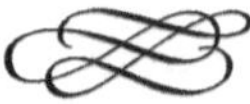

I didn't call anyone immediately after witnessing Pastor Clark's display of miracles at the church. I needed time to digest it. Besides, if I called Malene, she would've been all in knots about Claire's hand being healed.

Malene would, no doubt, have declared that Clark was Satan and we had to shove him back to Hades. Or she would be the first in line to have something on her body healed—like her sagging boobs.

And I didn't go to Rufus because he was dealing with his own PR mess. There was no telling what the fallout would be from the puppy fiasco, so I didn't want to burden him with anything else.

Which meant that I was forced to burden myself, basically.

"You know, I think my tail could be a little longer," Lady told me the next morning. "Do you think that pastor could heal it?"

"That's not what healing is."

"Oh." She thought about that. "Then, what is it?"

"You have to hurt or be wounded. It has to be something that science can't mend."

"Well, science cain't make my tail any longer."

I shook my head. "You're missing the point."

"No, I think you are."

A laugh bubbled from my throat. "Oh, you think so?"

"I *know* so." She padded over to where I sat on the couch, putting my shoes on. "So. What're we doing today?"

"*I'm* heading out to a job."

"Can I come?"

"I don't know. According to Liam, the construction site's a mess."

Liam was my contractor and all-around amazing guy. We'd never dated because he'd always been more like a brother to me than a love interest.

"That's okay," she said. "I like messes. I won't get in the way."

I rose. "Okay, if you promise to be good."

"I swear on my dead mother's grave that I'll be good."

"Your mother's not even dead. She lives two hours away."

Lady scoffed. "Well, whatever. You know what I mean."

I scooped her into my arms and we headed out.

First stop, Bender's Coffee. I needed a hot mocha like no one's business. As soon as I walked in, I spotted a line snaking from the counter and winding nearly all the way to the door.

"Looks like it's gonna be a wait," I murmured to Lady.

She nodded, knowing that I didn't like her to talk in public. Why bring on undue attention? And now, with Rufus being under the microscope, it was best not to even breathe about magic.

It took about five minutes before Lady and I reached the counter. Julie's hair had been pulled back into a scarf, but a few strands poked out. They matched the frazzled look on her face.

"Busy today," I said.

"My goodness, yes. I've never seen the place so slammed. No idea what's causing it other than Trina makes one heck of a cup of coffee."

I smiled. "I'm sure that's it. But I don't want to keep you, so I'll have my usual and a dog treat if you've got one."

"Sure do. Coming right up."

I paid and stepped into the line of folks waiting for coffee. While I was there, I overheard two women talking.

"Oh, she just makes the best cup, doesn't she?" said a woman wearing an emerald-green V-necked flowing blouse over a pair of white chinos. "I wake up every morning craving one."

The other woman, who was a little older, maybe in her forties, with short reddish hair and wearing a light blue sweater and glasses, replied,

"You're right. Ever since Trina moved in, I've just been wanting coffee like I never have before. Why, my Stanley says that I've become another person."

Both women laughed, but I couldn't help wondering if her Stanley was the one from the Guthrie's incident. "Excuse me."

"Yes?" the second woman said.

"I wasn't trying to eavesdrop, but I was wondering if your Stanley was the same man who was at the new sporting goods store the other day, the day when that Roy threatened everyone?"

"Why yes, that was him. Why? Were you there?"

"I was, actually."

She grasped my hand. "Oh dear. Are you okay?"

"Actually, I was wondering if Stanley was okay."

"Yes, he is. I know how the news is painting those events, but if it hadn't been for Rufus Mayes, then Stanley might not be with us anymore." Tears filled her eyes. "I owe that man a debt of gratitude."

"I know Rufus, and I'm sure he would say that you don't owe him anything. He was only doing what anyone would have done."

She smirked. "But they didn't, did they? No one else stood up to help. If you see him, please thank him for me."

"I would be happy to." Trina called out the name of a drink, and the woman said, "It looks like I'm up. It was nice talking to you, um…"

"Clementine. Clementine Cooke."

"Well, I'm Janie, and I'm in the phone book if you ever need me."

"Thank you, Janie."

She took her drink, and only a moment later, Trina said, "Medium mocha."

"That's me."

Trina placed the paper cup on the counter. "Hey, Clem, how're you?"

"Good. How're you?" I asked, seeing the mass of cups with the orders written in black ink beside her.

"Oh, I'm busy," she replied with a sigh. "But it's a good kind of busy. I love being in the middle of everything."

"Looks like everyone is loving you as the new barista." I took my drink and sipped it. It was heaven. Rich chocolate hit my tongue before sliding down my throat. The flavor mingled with the earthiness of the coffee, and both left their mark on my tastebuds, making me want more. "This is heaven."

"Aw, I'm so glad you like it." She started to make the next customer's order. "Seems you've got company."

She wasn't kidding. People in the coffee shop were smiling and lifting their cups to one another. They weren't just grabbing a cup of coffee and heading off to work. They were taking the time to savor their drinks.

"They really like what you make," I murmured, taking another sip. Oh, it was so good that I could've drained the whole cup with one gulp and asked for another.

But I was a lady. I didn't gobble things.

"Thanks for coming," Trina said.

"You're welcome," I replied, humming as I made my way slowly through the crowd.

I didn't know what it was, but I felt a buzzing in me, as if I glowed from the inside out. Suddenly I realized it would be more fun to sit in the coffee shop and chitchat with people than it would be to head down to a dusty old construction site.

I pulled out a chair and sat. Lady stared up at me. Out of one corner of her mouth she said, "What are you doing?"

I dropped my chin into my hand and stared at her. "Um, why are you whispering like that?"

Her gaze darted from left to right. "Because you've always told me not to talk in public."

"What public?" I gestured toward the folks in Bender's. "These people aren't the public. They're our friends."

She eyed me suspiciously. "Are you feeling okay?"

"Okay?" I considered the word. *Okay* did not do justice to how I felt. "I'm more than okay. I'm great. I feel wonderful." I caught the gaze of a mother with a stroller and pushed up beside her. "Are you okay, or are you great?"

She lifted her coffee cup. "I'm great! I'm better than okay."

"See?" I said to Lady. "She's great. I'm great. If I had to bet on it, I would say that everyone in this shop is great."

"I'm great," a man who'd been staring at his computer said.

"Me too," said a woman who was dressed in a pink satin blouse and black capri dress pants. "I'm wonderful."

I snapped my fingers. "That's another word for how I feel—wonderful. I feel great. I feel wonderful. I feel so many things."

All the colors in the room were intensified a hundredfold. The reds were sharper, the blues brighter, the yellows as cheery as the sun. It was intense.

And the feeling filling up my chest was wonderous, too. It was like my whole being was chock-full of love and happiness. I wanted to share it with the world.

I fished my phone from my purse and dialed Rufus. "Hey," he said in his husky voice.

"Hey," I said in return. My free finger, as if acting on its own, started twirling my hair in a flirtatious manner. "How're you?"

"Oh, you know, trying to avoid the television crews, and Tuney Sluggs, who I feel like might be trying to pin the car accident on me. I've done my best to convey that the puppies were an act of God—or Malene, for that matter—but I'm not sure he's buying it."

"Well, tell him to stick a fork in it, because you're done."

"Sorry?"

"What I mean is"—I was talking heavily into the phone now—"don't worry about it. But you know what you should worry about?"

"What's that?"

"Nothing." I laughed. "You should worry about nothing. There should be nothing bothering that handsome head of yours. In fact, you should come join me and we can worry about nothing together."

"Clearers? We should be worried about them."

"Clearers, shmearers. I don't think they're anything for us to concern our heads with. We should go out, enjoy the day, take Lady to a carnival and win a big stuffed teddy bear for her."

"Clem, are you feeling all right?"

"I'm feeling amazing." I blew a pesky stray hair from my face. "I feel great. I think," I dropped my voice to a whisper, "that we should really get to know one another better. Like, maybe I should come over to your place. Right now."

"Have you been drinking?"

"What? No. It's eight in the morning. But you know what I *could* drink up? Your love."

He paused and I thought that maybe I heard him cover his mouth and chuckle. "Where are you?"

He was taking me up on my offer to get busy! "I'm at Bender's."

"I'm coming to get you. Right now. Stay put."

"Yes, sir." I hung up the phone and smiled at Lady. "Me and Rufus are going to get busy, which means that I will be dropping you off at my house. Or maybe Malene's."

"Clem, you're not acting right," Lady whispered.

Gosh, I was so tired of hiding Lady, of being such a big fuddy-duddy and telling her not to talk in public. Who cared? What was the worst that could happen? The world would know that I had a talking dog and they would love her. I could just see it now—we'd go on talk shows and make appearances at big corporate events. Lady would be the keynote speaker at company yearly retreats. She would inspire folks by telling them that if she could overcome her inability to talk, they could do whatever they dreamed of!

So it was a minor inconvenience that magic had put her in that position. But so what? The important part of her story was that Lady could motivate the masses. I was certain of it.

"Clem, we should go," she murmured. "You need to go home."

"Rufus is coming."

"We'll meet him there."

I cupped a hand to my ear. "What was that?"

"We'll meet him there," she repeated.

"What was that? I couldn't hear you. Speak up."

Lady's eyes narrowed as if she was on to me, and then she opened her mouth just as the dining room quieted and shouted, "I said, we'll meet him there!"

All gazes turned to us, and everyone seemed to zero in on Lady. I smiled. This was great!

I pointed to my dog. "She can talk, y'all!"

A teenager lifted from his chair. "I got it on video! I'm going to break TikTok!"

I grinned down at Lady, who was shaking with fear. "You're going to be famous. Smile for the camera!"

CHAPTER 10

$\mathcal{I}$ wasn't on TikTok, so I didn't know if Lady had actually broken the Internet, but I did know that as soon as folks saw her speak, they all wanted a picture with her.

"Sure," I said with a giggle. "Let's do pics."

We'd sat for half a dozen before Rufus entered.

I waved. "And there he is, my handsome man. Y'all, don't be afraid. He was never going to hurt anyone with magic. Don't believe what those foolish reporters say. They've gone and lost their minds thinking that Rufus Mayes could hurt anyone." And then I remembered, "And did any of y'all see him with the puppies? That was the cutest photo shoot ever." Rufus stood beside me, and I dragged my finger across his chest. "The only thing that would've made it better was if he hadn't had his shirt on and we could have all seen his marble godlike chest." A woman was listening with interest so I placed a hand to my mouth and whispered, "I've seen it. It's amazing."

Rufus curled his fingers around my bicep. "Come on, let's go."

"But these are my new friends," I whined. "I can't leave them."

"You can and you will. Let's go."

He dragged me off and he was so strong that I couldn't resist. Plus, I knew what was going to happen once we were alone, so I had a mountain of motivation to leave with him.

He didn't speak as he tugged me to his SUV and stowed me and Lady safely inside. But once he was in and he started the ignition—

"Whoa, look at all those colors." I ran my hands over the dashboard and admired how bright and colorful all the lights were. "This is the pips."

Rufus put the vehicle into drive, and we rumbled down the road. He turned to me. "What did she take?"

"Who? Lady? She didn't take anything unless you count the bundles of love that I give her." I hugged the little booger to my chest. "A world of hugs is what I gave her."

"Lady," Rufus corrected. "What has Clementine taken?"

"She didn't start acting weird until she drank that." Lady pointed her nose to the cup I was still holding. It was half full of liquid. I wanted to make that drink last forever, it was so delicious. "Come to think of it, a lot of folks in that coffee shop were acting weird."

"How?" he asked.

"They were talking to one another."

Rufus quirked a brow. "In a coffee shop at eight in the morning?"

"Yep, they sure were. Strangest thing I ever saw. Even two ladies waiting in line for their drinks were talking about how they couldn't get enough of the place."

I lifted my cup. "I know. It's all so good."

Rufus plucked the cup from my hand. "Not now. You can have more later."

I reached for it, but he placed it by the window, where I couldn't get it. "But it's mine."

"And you can have more of it, but not right now." After I dropped my hand to my lap, he asked, "Did anything else happen?"

"I spoke in front of folks. I think Clem planned it that way."

I giggled. "It was so awesome. You should have seen it. Everyone was amazed that Lady could talk. And it's going to be on TikTok!" I clapped in delight. "The whole world is going to see that Lady has real actual speaking ability."

Rufus glared at me. "What is wrong with you?"

"What?" I asked, hurt.

"Don't you think we have enough problems right now? The world discovers that you have a talking dog and our lives here could go down-hill faster than you can snap your fingers."

I snapped my fingers. "Look. The world didn't implode."

"But it will. Now let's get you to my place and see what sort of spell you're under."

"Spell? I'm not under a spell."

He smirked. "Right. You're not under a spell. Well, you don't smell of alcohol, and you were served a drink by a witch, so my next best guess is, spell."

I blew air between my lips, vibrating them. "Fine. I'm under a spell. Whatever."

We arrived at Rufus's and he made sure to keep the cup far, far out of my reach, which I deemed completely unfair. I wouldn't keep his mocha from him if he had one.

As soon as we were inside, he fished what looked like a black rock from a jar and handed it to me. "Eat that."

"It looks like a dog turd."

Lady sniffed it. "It ain't. Trust me, I know that smell from a mile away."

I lifted my nose. "I'm not eating it."

"It's charcoal. It'll absorb whatever potion you drank."

"What if I don't want it to absorb the potion?"

"Then I'm afraid that I can't be responsible for how long you'll be walking around with your judgment impaired."

I crossed my arms. "My judgment isn't impaired."

He rolled his eyes. "Right. You just let the world see that your dog can talk and you're of sound mind."

"And body." I grinned and walked my fingers up his arm. "Which reminds me…"

"Not until you eat this."

"Fine." I shoved the whole thing in my mouth and chewed. And wanted to vomit. "Oh. My. Gosh. This is horrible."

"Yes, and that horrible thing is going to cure you," he snapped.

His face was pinched in frustration. I didn't understand why he was angry. He wasn't the one eating the horrible charcoal. Yuck. It tasted exactly like you would imagine—like dirt that had been compressed and stuck together with a dash of disgusting.

But I chewed and I chewed.

"You have to swallow it," he said over his shoulder while he worked some sort of big bad potion that would uncover the mystery of what had happened to me. I had news for him—there was no mystery. I was simply in love with life. That was all. End of story.

"Keep eating it," Lady encouraged.

That was easy for her to say. She was a dog, and everyone knew that dogs ate poop on a regular basis. So she would literally eat *anything* and like it.

But even though I wanted to vomit, I did as I was told, chewing and swallowing the charcoal. Within minutes the headiness faded and I was left feeling normal.

Which was sort of boring when I thought about it.

Rufus glanced up from his worktable. "Feeling better?"

"Yes. Is there anything that I can help you with?"

"I don't think so." His sleeves were rolled to his elbows, and he was hunched over a book. "The best thing for you to do is rest."

"But I'd like to help."

He smirked and glanced over to Lady. "Do you think that she can be trusted enough to help?"

"I don't know," my dog said with a sniff. "She's been awfully ornery for the past hour. I'm not even sure I know who she is anymore."

My jaw unhinged. "What do you mean, you don't know who I am? I'm Clem. The same person that I've always been."

"I think what she means to say"—Rufus walked around to the front of the table and rested the back of his legs on it—"is that you were acting well out of character, and she's not sure if you're back to your old self."

"Exactly." Lady gave a hard nod. "Are you Clem or are you the woman overtaken with the potion?"

"I wasn't…okay, I was. But I couldn't help it." I threw up my hands in frustration. "It wasn't like I had any control over what I was doing."

Lady shot me a pointed look. "Is that so?"

"Yes, tell us what you experienced," Rufus encouraged.

"Well, as soon as I sipped the drink, I felt lighter, as if I had no worries. And the world was very colorful. It was like I'd been missing out on the depth of color my entire life. I didn't understand it. And I just felt free. There was nothing to worry about, and no *reason* to be worried because everything was going to be all right."

"Sounds like you were on drugs," Lady said sadly. "I never thought I'd see the day when my mama fell under the influence of smack."

"Lady, I didn't do smack."

She shook her head in disappointment. "You might as well have from the way that you're describing it."

"I think we can safely say that Clementine had no control over what occurred," Rufus explained.

"Say what you want, but I still believe you did some smack."

I nearly slapped my forehead I was so frustrated. "Lady, do you even know what that is?"

"I've watched enough police shows to be well versed in street lingo," she informed me.

"If you say so."

A potion behind Rufus bubbled. The sound caught his attention, and he glanced over his shoulder. "Looks like it's ready." He clapped his hands and walked lithely around the desk, talking as he went. "Obviously I knew something was wrong when you called me. On my way to pick you up, I quickly devised this test."

I rose from the overstuffed velvet-draped chair that I was sitting in and crossed to him. Rufus had a flair for the gothic, and I liked it.

"What are you looking for?" I asked.

"Mainly what sort of substance that you were dosed with," he said, his expression grim.

I hated to tell him, but I already knew the answer. I hadn't been dosed with anything. I'd watched Trina make my drink, and she hadn't put anything extra in it. All she'd done was drop the chocolate in, added the coffee, and then whipped the milk.

Wait. The chocolate. What if it hadn't been chocolate? But as quickly as the thought came to me, I dismissed it. No. Trina was on the up-and-up. I was certain of it.

Rufus held the vial with a mitt and added a sprinkle of crushed eggshells to the open mouth. The eggshells reacted with the reagent in the vial, and the potion bubbled over before stopping. The color of the liquid turned clear and became very still.

"What does that mean?"

Rufus placed the beaker on the desk. "It means that nothing was added into your drink."

"That's what I thought," I said proudly. Don't ask me what there was to be proud of except for the fact that I'd been right. "Trina didn't dose me."

"Then what did she do?" Lady asked. "Did she spit in it?"

"Ew. No, and don't say that, please."

Lady babbled on. "Well, that witch did something. I know it. You were perfectly normal when you walked in, and by the time we were leaving, you were selling me down the river."

"I was no—" She glared at me, and I shut my mouth. Okay, yes, I might've sold my dog down the river. "It was an accident?" I said, more a question than statement.

"Right. An accident," she spat.

"What this means, I'm afraid," Rufus interjected, "is that your friend Trina, who made the drink, is somehow filling the cups with magic. Now, whether it's intentional or not is something that we need to find out. Because the amount of control that she just exerted on you, if given to a regular person, could influence them."

"To hate us," I whispered, realizing the magnitude of our problem.

"Exactly," he said.

My phone rang and I slipped it from my pocket. "Oh, it's Malene. Hello?"

"What's this I see about Lady talking?" she yelled.

My stomach folded in half. What had I done? "Is it on the news or something?"

"Worse," she said.

What could've been worse than the news? "How's it worse?"

"I just got a call from the church ladies. They saw it on Facebook. Everyone knows. What have you done, Clem?"

My heart sank. What had I done? And how, just how was I going to make this right?

CHAPTER 11

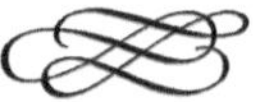

$\mathcal{B}$y the time Sunday rolled around, I'd had no choice but to turn my phone's ringer off as people were blowing my phone up left and right. If I'd thought that the world had gone crazy over what had happened with Rufus in the gun shop, then the world had actually lost its mind over Lady.

Everywhere we went, my dog drew attention. People wanted her autograph, or they wanted to hear her say something, anything, so that they could post it on the Internet and get all the glory.

And Lady, though she'd been terrified at first (since I'd told her that the government would steal her and work experiments on her body ala *E.T. the Extraterrestrial*), she had quickly settled into her newfound celebrity.

"Where are my sunglasses?" she said right before we left for church on Sunday.

"Your sunglasses?" The request flabbergasted me. "You don't have sunglasses."

She padded over and stared at me in dismay. "Well, don't you think that I need some? The sun is bad for your eyes, Clem. I cain't be going blind. What would my fans do?"

I scoffed. "Your fans would probably carry you wherever you wanted to go."

"Exactly. But what if one of them drops me and I wind up shattering my leg bone? And the surgeon who's always had good luck repairing bones suddenly cain't fix mine? What then, Clem? *What then?*"

What then was that I would need a drink in order to deal with my dog's inflated ego. "Um, I don't believe things will get that far."

She crossed to my purse and crawled inside. "You're taking me to church, right?"

Two days earlier, I'd caught someone trying to open a window when I'd stepped out for a few minutes. All to get a look at Lady. Ever since then, I didn't leave her at home. She went everywhere that I did.

"You can come, but you can't come out of the purse. There aren't supposed to be dogs in church."

She frowned. "Why would God keep all his children from worshipping him?"

I rolled my eyes. "Well, to be technical, you're a dog. Not a human. I don't think the rules about church and God apply to you."

"But I am a soul, Clem. Doesn't that account for anything?" she pleaded.

"Just get in the purse."

"Okay."

A car horn beeped from outside. No doubt it was Malene. She was the only person I knew who would blow their horn even on a Sunday morning, when plenty of folks slept in.

I grabbed my purse and stepped outside.

"We gotta get a move on," Malene shouted from her Miata, "or all the good seats will be gone."

"I'm coming!" I locked up and headed down the stairs and into the car. "What about Willard?"

My grandmother checked her appearance in the rearview mirror. She cleaned a line of red lipstick from one corner of her mouth. "He's meeting us there. And Rufus?"

"He's meeting us there as well."

She smirked. "Oh, you finally talked him into coming?"

"With everything that happened this week with Lady, he wants to make sure that we're safe."

"It's been a busy news week cycle. Now hold on. I don't want to be late."

Malene slammed her foot against the accelerator and we sped off. Not only was she the only person I knew who honked her horn on a Sunday, but she was also a speeder, having no guilt about breaking the limit on her way through town.

When I asked her about it, she just replied, "Those signs are only a suggestion. When you get as old as me, you don't consider the posted limit a rule anymore."

Whatever she said. When we arrived at church, the parking lot was filling up fast.

"Is it Easter and I just don't know it?" she said.

"What do you mean?"

"The lot's never full at this time." Malene pointed to the cars. "There are only a few open spots. I'd better call Willard and warn him."

She called him after sliding into an open space and I got out to wait. As soon as my foot hit the asphalt, a group of people saw me and started murmuring. No doubt they were talking about Lady. But for once they just kept walking, not bothering to ask me a gazillion questions.

Lady stuck her nose out of my purse far enough to notice it, too. "Why ain't my fans coming to see me?"

"Because," I whispered harshly, "they don't know that you're here."

"We should let them see me," she said.

"I already told you, there are no dogs allowed in church."

Malene got out of the Miata. "Y'all ready? We gotta beat Claire to the good seats."

Oh crap. That reminded me about what had happened with Claire earlier in the week. With all the commotion surrounding Lady, I'd completely forgotten about it.

"Malene, there's something I need to—"

"Would you look at that," my grandmother said.

"What?"

She pointed to a sign hanging beside the front door that showcased a golden retriever. "Looks like pets are now welcome in church."

"What?" Lady's head popped up from the depths of my purse. "What did you say?"

"Let me read it to you—all creatures great and small are welcome to every service here at First Baptist. And look, there's a picture of a dog."

"Whoopee, Clem! My fans can now be in my presence. Get me out of here!"

Malene elbowed me. "Yeah, Clem. Get your dog out and let them all bask in her celebrity."

I did not want to do that. But if I didn't, Lady would just start talking loudly, which would shift all focus to her, anyway.

So I pulled her out of my bag and took the leash that I kept in my purse and attached it to her collar. "Okay, remember: be cool."

"I'd be cooler if I was wearing sunglasses," she told me.

I ignored her. But as soon as I put her on the ground, people were coming up to us, oohing and ahhing over the dog.

"I knew that you should have gotten me sunglasses," she murmured. To her adoring fans, Lady said, "Y'all, I'm only here for church. I don't want to take away from what God has to teach us. But I will be available for pictures and paw prints after the service."

I rolled my eyes. A monster had been created out of my once humble dog. Oh, who was I kidding? Lady had never been humble. But at least she hadn't had an out-of-control ego.

We went inside and found the pew that Norma Ray and Urleen had saved for us.

"You made it just in time," Urleen said. "Someone"—she wiggled her brows—"was eyeing your seats."

"Now who could that have been?" Malene said sarcastically. Her gaze swept around for a moment before stopping. "I'm sure we've got Claire to blame that on."

"And how," Norma Ray whispered. "She was chomping at the bit to take your spots."

"Malene." We all glanced over our shoulders as Claire reached our pew. "You got the best seat again."

"It helps to have friends in high places."

"Or low ones." Claire's gaze dragged over all of us. She lifted her left hand and brushed her hair from her face.

Malene sucked air. "What happened to you?"

"What are you talking about?" Claire said, her voice dripping with faux innocence. "I haven't the slightest idea what you mean."

"You know exactly what I mean. Your...your...your hand. What happened to it? It looks like someone put it on a stretcher and yanked it right."

Claire's eyes narrowed. "Well, it looks like the great Malene Fredericks doesn't know everything, now does she? She's not privy to every piece of information that goes on in this town."

I couldn't see Malene's face, but I didn't have to, to know that it was a deep shade of crimson. "Never you mind, Claire. I know what happened; I just wanted you to think that I didn't."

A throaty laugh erupted from Claire's mouth. "Right. I'm sure that you do. Anyway, y'all will find out soon enough."

She sauntered off and soon as she was out of earshot, Malene leaned over. "Who knew about this? Did any of y'all?"

"Not me." Norma Ray slashed her finger over her chest. "Cross my heart and hope to die."

"Sticking a needle in your eye might improve your vision," Malene quipped.

Norma Ray glared at her.

Urleen patted her shoulder. "Now, now. We're all friends here. Let's be kind to one another. But no, I didn't know a thing about Claire."

"What about you, Clem?" Malene asked.

Oh no. My grandmother would kill me if she knew the truth—that I'd forgotten to blab about the biggest news since forever.

But luckily I was saved by a tall, handsome man.

"Rufus!" I reached over Malene toward him. "You made it."

"The parking's terrible today." He kissed my cheek. "Have I missed anything?"

"No, no. Excuse me." I brushed past Malene and took a spot beside Rufus. "You're just in time."

"Is there room for me?" Willard asked, appearing behind Rufus.

"Yes, come on in," Malene said to him. To me, she added finger jabbing the air. "This isn't finished, Clem. I know you're hiding something."

Willard opened his mouth, I was sure to ask what I was hiding, when the sanctuary went dark. All the lights flickered out and several people gasped. A second later, three spotlights flared to life. They flew up and down the stage as an announcer (probably one of the deacons) said into a microphone, "Ladies and gentlemen, please stand on your feet as we sing in praise to the Lord."

Next thing I knew, a band appeared onstage. Not a choir, but a band! And the lead guitarist strummed out a contemporary Christian song. I was anticipating that the hair of all the blue-tressed old ladies would turn white with shock.

But it didn't happen, and the band rocked several Christian songs as the old folks looked around, confused as to what the heck had happened to their calm Christian music sung by the choir and accompanied by the organ.

All of that was gone, and in its place was First Baptist 2.0.

When we finished the last song, the guitarist lifted his hand in worship. "And now, I want to announce our pastor for the day, Brother Clark!"

The band erupted in applause, and so did half of the sanctuary. The three spotlights started swirling around again, all fancy-like, and out trotted Pastor Clark, waving to the crowd like we were in a stadium and he was on the jumbotron.

Once the applause died down, he spoke, his face beaming, eyes bright with happiness. "Good morning, Peachwood! I am so blessed to be able to preach to y'all again. Let's first say a prayer for Brother Steve's family, whose mother is still sick."

"Sick my foot," Malene grumbled.

I shot her a dark look and she shrugged. "What?"

"Can you be quiet? We're in church."

She smirked, looking like she had an awful lot to say, but managed to keep silent.

After Brother Clark led us in prayer, he held out his arms. "I suppose plenty of y'all know what's been happening in our small town."

"No, we don't," Malene grumbled, and a few folks laughed.

Clark, totally unruffled, clapped his hands together. "Well, looks like news hasn't spread to everyone. In that case, let me fill those of y'all who don't know in on our not-so-little secret."

"That would be great," Malene replied.

Her comments were beginning to be embarrassing. Even Rufus leaned over. "Is she always like this in church? So chatty?"

"No," I murmured. "She's not like that at all. She's bothered today."

Clark continued. "There are miracles happening here in Peachwood. Great things have occurred here. Wonderful things. Such fascinating things that you won't believe them unless you see them. God is doing his work. He's granted me the ability to heal his children. If you have an ailment, I want to heal you. *God* wants to heal you. He wants you to become whole, so that you can reach your full physical potential. So tell me—who wants to be healed? Who wants to help me do God's work?"

The room was silent, and then Malene's hand shot up. "I do! I want you to heal me."

Clark gestured toward her. "Then come on up here and let's see what God can do."

CHAPTER 12

My heart raced. What was Malene doing? Clark wanted to heal people with actual problems, not crazy old women.

Malene brushed past me on her way to the end of the pew. "Excuse me, I have some healing to get done."

"What are you thinking?"

"I'm thinking that I want to be healed," she spat back. "Now, get out of my way." When I didn't move, she added, "You don't want to stand between me and God, now do you?"

I rolled my eyes and shrank back, letting her pass. Nobody wanted to be told that they were standing in the path of God for the wrong reasons.

Clark took her hand. "Thank you for doing this. For believing."

"You're welcome," Malene said stiffly.

Willard leaned over to me. "Clem, what has gotten into her?"

"I don't know. I feel like she wants to prove a point."

"Oh, she wants to prove a point, all right," he said bitterly. "But I'm not sure if it's the kind she thinks."

I had no idea what that meant and was about to ask him when Brother Clark spoke. "For those of you who are uncertain of the miracles, let me introduce you to someone. Claire, would you please come up here."

Boy, did Malene ever give Claire the stink eye as she made her way to the front of the sanctuary. I couldn't be certain, but Claire may have volleyed it right back.

"Come up here," Clark said. "Don't be shy."

"Oh, she's not shy," Malene said.

Claire's face looked like she'd just sucked on a lemon. But instead of saying anything nasty to Malene, she smiled at Brother Clark. "Here I am."

"Sister Claire, you've been part of this church family for a long time, am I right?"

"For two decades."

He nodded. "So these good people here would be familiar with your affliction."

"My hand has been shriveled my entire life."

He smiled kindly. "And how is it now?"

She lifted it high so that those in the back could see. "Now it's healed. I've been healed by the power of God acting through you, Brother Clark!"

Oohs and aahs filled the sanctuary. People whispered to one another. I heard words like *miracle, impossible, amazing.*

"Did you know about this?" Rufus asked me.

"Oh, Clem knew. We both did," Lady said. "We saw it happen the other night."

"I forgot to tell you," I explained. "The next day was when I drank that loopy potion that wasn't a potion."

"Ah, I see," he replied.

"And how do you feel?" Clark asked Claire. "Since God has done his work through you?"

"I feel blessed," she announced happily. "I feel like a whole new woman, one picked by God to do his work, to spread his gospel."

Everyone clapped and Clark let Claire return to her seat. "But folks, that isn't all. We're doing amazing work here at First Baptist, and I want you to see it for yourselves. Starting with you," he said to Malene. "I want the entire congregation to see God's will worked inside of you. Please, tell all of us what afflicts you."

Malene frowned. *Yes, Malene,* I wanted to yell. *Tell us your ailments.*

As far as I knew, other than being old and cranky, my grandmother didn't have any ailments. But those two were quite enough.

"I have doubts," she explained.

"About what? About God?" Clark asked.

"About what you did to Claire. I have serious doubts."

He laughed. "Well, let's heal you of those doubts, shall we? Let's allow the Lord's power to flow through you and cast those dark thoughts right from your head, as Jesus cast Legion from the man."

She looked at him crossly. "I'm not possessed by demons."

"But what's worse is that you're possessed with doubt." He faced the crowd. "Everyone, what is the one thing that we need as Christians? Faith. Belief. There is no room in our hearts for second-guessing. There can be none of that. We must be filled with absolute, staunch fire for God. Am I right?"

"Amen," someone shouted from the back.

Clark held his arms open to Malene. "Are you ready to be purged from your affliction?"

"I don't know."

"Are you?" he said like he was asking a child.

"I guess so."

"Then let God's power banish your disbelief."

"Yes," she murmured.

Her attitude was so sour that I wanted to die. When I glanced over at Urleen and Norma Ray, both women had their heads down as if they were terribly embarrassed, too. It was unthinkable. Why was Malene doing this? I had half a mind to rush the stage and pull her down lickety-split.

Clark placed both hands on her shoulders. "Malene Fredericks, close your eyes." I was surprised when she did so without argument. "Let's pray. God, I ask that you see this woman and that you touch her with your healing hand. Of all the things that we as Christians must have, it's belief. No, she has no physical wounds, but I ask that you heal the tears on her heart. Mend them so that she can truly see. In your name, amen. You may open your eyes."

Malene did so slowly. She glanced around the sanctuary, looking from face to face, a question in her eyes as if she was trying to decipher something.

"How do you feel?" Clark asked.

"Why, I feel…healed. I can see! I have the faith of a thousand Christians. You can heal hearts and bodies. Why, I feel such love. I love all of you. I even love you, Claire."

"It's a miracle," Norma Ray shouted. "Malene loves Claire!"

Malene stepped from the dais spryly. She had a bit too much energy, and I worried that she might break a leg coming down.

"Be careful," Clark warned. "Now, all of you have seen how God is working through me. Now. I ask you—who needs to be healed? Who has an ailment, a sickness, a broken heart and needs to be washed in the power of Christ?" Suddenly, just about every hand in the sanctuary flew up! Clark smiled as if that was what he'd been expecting. "Come on, everyone. Come down slowly and let's get to work."

The next two hours flew by. Normally if the sermon lasted over thirty minutes people were getting antsy to leave. But that wasn't the case that Sunday. Folks couldn't get enough of Pastor Clark and his healing abilities.

He healed everyone—from a man who'd been deaf his entire life to a little boy in a wheelchair and everyone in between. It was shocking and strange and…absolutely wonderful.

As we were leaving the church, surrounded by a throng of people, Lady piped up, "Y'all, I'm still here if anyone wants a picture or my paw print! I'm here!"

But folks raced right on by her, gibbering about the miracles that they'd witnessed. I couldn't see my dog's face, but I had a feeling that was quite a blow to her brittle ego.

"Tell us, Malene," Norma Ray said, "is what you said up there on the stage true? Do you really love everyone?"

"Norma, I can even put up with your stupidity and it won't bother me." Malene embraced her. "You are a special child of God."

"I'm not sure if I'm supposed to be hurt by that or feel good," Norma Ray replied in confusion.

"I think you're supposed to wonder what in the world happened back there," Urleen said.

"Wonder is right," Willard added. "I've never seen anything like that in my entire life. What a spectacle. It's too bad that Pastor Steve hasn't been here to see what's going on in his church."

"Unless that was the plan to begin with." Rufus slid his hands into his pockets. "It does seem strange. The timing, I mean."

"We don't know exactly where Clark came from," Willard added.

"What are you two grumbling about?" Malene asked. "He's performing miracles in there. I'm healed. Nothing can bother me today or ever. He's a good Christian man doing God's work. Why, he even healed Claire. And did you see him get the man in the wheelchair to walk?" She clasped her hands. "It was a sight."

A sight of what, though? "Beware false prophets," I reminded her.

"Clem, you just need to see," she told me. "You haven't been healed by Clark. When you are, you'll see what I mean. You'll see that what he's doing is right and wonderful."

I glanced at Rufus, whose jaw jumped. "No one doubts his power, Malene. He's certainly healing people. But is it God's gift?"

"Of course it is," she snapped. "What else could it be?"

Magic. That was what else. Very powerful magic. The kind that a clearer could create.

"I just think we need to be careful," I said.

"Careful of what?" my grandmother asked. We'd reached the car and hit the button on the fob, unlocking the doors. "What on earth is there to be careful of?"

"We don't know Clark, and he did appear all of a sudden."

"Clem, you can't plan when a miracle will come to you. If there's anything in life that I've learned, it's that. They just appear and you have to do your part and be open to them."

Who was this woman? "All I'm saying is that we need to look before we leap."

"I agree," Rufus said. "If you go see Pastor Clark or come to the church, let us know."

Malene opened her car door. "Why should I do that? I'm a grown woman, healed of all my fear and spite."

Norma Ray piped up. "Just so that we can come with you. I want to be healed, too."

"Me too," Urleen added, sneaking me a wink that Malene didn't catch.

"Well, why didn't y'all get healed today?" Before they could answer, Malene shook her head. "Never mind. Clark was too busy healing those who were truly needy. Well, if I go to the church, I'll let you know. Now, if there's nothing else, I need to get home. There's some chicken salad in my refrigerator calling to me."

"You can ride with me," Rufus said to me.

We said goodbye to Malene, and I watched her speed away in the car, waving to folks she would normally ignore. As far as being a good Christian went, perhaps whatever Clark had done was a plus. Still, something didn't sit right in my stomach.

Willard came over, a shadow covering his eyes. "I don't know about y'all, but I'm skeptical about Pastor Clark."

"Which part, exactly?" Rufus said. "The one where he heals folks or the fact that his healing has worked so well on Malene?"

"All of it." Willard sounded grim and looked even grimmer. "I'm not sure what to do about her."

"There's only one thing that we can do," Rufus said.

"What's that?" I asked.

"Find out if Clark is the real deal."

"What are you suggesting?" Willard asked.

Rufus scrubbed a hand down his cheek. "I'm not sure yet. But when I figure it out, I'll let you know."

"You may want to make that sooner rather than later." Urleen nodded down the street, where Malene was driving slowly, at least ten miles per hour below the limit. "Because my friend isn't right, and I want to fix her."

"Oh, I don't know," Norma Ray interjected. "I like this new Malene. She's so nice."

She might have been nice, but a Stepford wife had replaced my grandmother. If we didn't get the old Malene back, I had the feeling that we'd be stuck with the new and improved version.

Forever.

CHAPTER 13

$\mathcal{W}$illard promised to keep a close eye on Malene and inform us if any new developments occurred in her behavior. With church over, we all split up and headed home.

Lady sat in my lap as Rufus drove us down the road. "Why didn't any of my fan club come and see me?" she whined. "I was there in church. Surely they recognized me." My dog glanced over her shoulder. "Clem, you think that I need to wear sunglasses in order to appear more aloof? You know, so that folks realize that they're in the presence of a star?"

"Um, I think *not* wearing sunglasses is a great idea. Just stay the way you are."

Rufus draped his elbow on the lip of the door. "Something about that Brother Clark bothers me."

"You mean beside the fact that he showed up all of a sudden, right when we know the clearers are coming?"

"Yes, that would be one reason." He paused. "But it's very strange, don't you think? That a sporting goods shop opens run by a wizard, then a barista infuses happiness into her drinks and now there's a preacher healing the sick."

"A little bit too much of a coincidence?" I asked.

"Precisely." He slowed at a light and turned to face me. "If only one of those things had happened, I would say that's it, we've found our man. But it's almost as if so much is going on that someone wants to throw us off the scent."

"Too much of a good thing, huh?" Lady asked.

"Something like that," he murmured.

"Well for what it's worth," I told him. "I don't think Trina is any part of it. Yes, she creates magical drinks. But I suspect that she isn't aware of how potent they actually are."

"And what about the sporting goods store?"

"What about it?"

"Have you ever been in a store like that and encountered two men fighting?"

"No."

"Me neither." The light turned green, and Rufus pinned his focus back on the road. "It was strange that such a thing happened."

"Of course, I've only been in a sporting goods store a handful of times. Perhaps more fighting occurs than I know of."

"It doesn't." He gave me a pointed look. "I think that warrants some inspecting."

"Oh, are we going to investigate?" Lady said, tail wagging. "I do love doing some investigating. Clem, I'm going to need a black outfit and maybe a bandanna so that I can cover my head. Or better yet, how about a bandit mask? Yes, that'll work."

"Hold on there, dog. No one said anything about investigating."

"Rufus did. Didn't you?"

He grimaced. "It is sort of what I meant. But Lady, you're a celebrity now. You can't be expected to get your hands dirty."

She glanced over at him. "I know if it came right down to it, those Kardashian sisters would love to solve mysteries."

I scratched behind her ear. "I seriously doubt that."

"But that don't mean I cain't do it. Come on, Rufus! Who are we going to investigate first? The pastor or the gun shop? Or are we going to question Trina and find out exactly why she's putting magic into her drinks?"

"Let me think," he answered.

We reached my street, and Rufus turned down it. We stopped in front of my house, and Rufus killed the engine. "I suppose that there are several different directions we can go. However, all of this started with the sporting goods store. So I say we start there."

"What are we going to search for, exactly?" I asked, my voice thick with skepticism. "What happened was a one-time occurrence. It's not as if we can hang around the store and see if another fight breaks out. Besides, if one had, don't you think that we would have heard about it?"

"Perhaps. Perhaps not."

I didn't know what Rufus had in mind, but I didn't see how we could investigate the store. Brother Clark we could at least watch and follow. But the store—

"We'll follow the owner," I said, the idea striking me, "see where he goes, what he's up to."

Rufus smiled. "I knew that there was a reason that I liked you."

I laughed. "Hopefully more than one."

He leaned over and kissed me. Lady squeezed her body between us. "Okay, okay. Get a room, you two."

"What, you don't like us kissing?" I joked.

"Not when you're squishing me," she replied.

"That's fine. We need to save our energy anyway." Rufus opened his door. "For tonight."

I quirked a brow. "We're going to start following Jody that soon?"

"Why waste time?"

As he shut his door and came around to open mine, I wondered, why waste time, indeed?

❧

"Where is my black outfit?" Lady padded into my bedroom. "I told you that I needed it."

I was too busy picking out my own clothes to look up. "For the last time, you're not coming."

"And why not?" She padded over to my feet and pawed my leg. "I'm an integral part of this dynamic trio. I need to be there, Clem. You're gonna need me to be your watchdog."

"After no one paid attention to you in church today, I think you're safe to stay here. Besides, we'll be okay without you." I spotted the black

T-shirt that I'd been searching for and plucked it from my dresser drawer. "There. My outfit's complete."

"And what about mine?"

"I've already told you." I changed out of my lighter shirt and pulled on the dark one. "You're staying here. We can't have a dog with us when we're investigating."

"And why not?"

"Because you might bark."

She gasped. "How dare you offend me so badly. Who do you think I am, some normal off-the-street mutt?"

"No, of course not." I lifted her from the ground and hugged her tight. "I absolutely do not think that. However, I also know that you're a dog, and your instincts are strong. If you heard a strange sound, you would bark."

"Would not."

"Would too."

"Okay, I probably would."

"See? We can't have any disturbance, something that will give us away."

She gave me her sad puppy-dog eyes. "Is this one of those 'it's not you, it's me' instances?"

"No, this is definitely an 'it's you' occasion."

"Fine. But as long as you tell me everything that happens, I'll stay here."

As if she had a choice in the matter. My dog seemed to think that her way was the law when it came to my life, and nothing that I could say would convince her otherwise.

"Sure. I'll tell you everything."

"Thank you."

I put her down and finished changing clothes. I was nervous about tonight. I couldn't remember the last time that I'd spied on someone. The only picture that I had in my mind of doing the deed was us hanging out by a window and peering into it, trying to see what Jody might or might not have been doing that was surreptitious.

Whatever we found, I hoped that it gave us a good idea of what was really happening in town. Were the three new people connected, as

Rufus thought? Or were Jody, Trina and Clark all independent yet highly suspicious players?

Only time would tell.

I tugged on my dark jeans, jammed my feet into a pair of slip-on shoes, and was ready. I slid my phone into my back pocket and presented myself to Lady.

"How do I look?"

"Like you're about to go to the park and mime for money."

"Ha, ha, very funny. But seriously?"

She cocked her head to one side. "Don't you think that you're missing something?"

"What?"

"Your golden hammer."

"Oh no. Every time I use that thing, bad stuff happens."

That was true. The magic hammer was capable of fixing just about anything, but at a cost. Something else would break, and I didn't feel like having something else break on me while on a covert mission.

Not that we were playing *Mission: Impossible* or anything. We weren't exactly being covert, just sneaky.

"But Clem," Lady argued, "what if you need it? What if…?"

I placed a fist on my hip. "What if what?"

"What if you're standing under an eave of a building and the building is old, so old that it starts to cave on you. At the very last second, you touch the hammer to the house and the eave fixes itself, saving you from a gruesome death by smooshing."

"I highly doubt that'll happen. Besides, we can just use magic to sav—"

"And what if," she interrupted, "your truck breaks down right after you're spotted by some hillbillies, and they don't like the look of you, so they're chasing you. You get into your truck, but it won't start. It's only because of your hammer, which you touch to the dashboard and fix your vehicle, that you're able to escape to safety."

"I just don't think that's going to happ—"

"And what if," she nearly shouted, "you need to get closer to hear what a man is saying, but the porch boards of his house are covered in rusty nails that are poking through the wood. One wrong step and you've got tetanus. But with the help of the hammer, you're able to save yourself."

I lifted my hand for her to stop. "Okay, I get it. You want me to take the hammer. Is that it?"

"I would feel better if you did."

I supposed that it wouldn't matter if I explained that Rufus could just use magic to fix any of the circumstances that she had pitched to me. But instead of arguing (because arguing with Lady never helped anything), I marched into my closet and pulled out the shoebox where the hammer resided.

"That's a real secure system you got there," she said sarcastically.

I shot her a scathing look. "It works for me."

I pulled the hammer from the box and sucked air. It really was beautiful. The only magical object that I owned, the hammer was gold from top to bottom and weighed a good three pounds.

"Now, where am I going to hide it?"

"Down your pants," she said.

My jaw dropped. "You've got to be kidding."

"I ain't kidding. How else are you gonna keep people from seeing it? You put it in your back pocket and someone could spy the gold. So either you put it down your pants or inside your bra."

"This isn't a dollar bill. I can't just stuff it in my bra."

"Then down the pants it is," she said with a certain amount of satisfaction that was unsettling. "I'll watch while you do it."

Great. Just what I wanted, to have my dog eye me while I performed humiliating acts. "I'll do it in the bathroom."

"Suit yourself."

And that was exactly what I did. I went into the bathroom and pushed the hammer down the front of my pants. It was uncomfortable, poking me in the wrong parts. So I moved it to the back and that worked out better, though the metal was cold.

When I exited the bathroom, I lifted my hands. "Ta-da! All set?"

Lady pranced around me, cocking her head one way and then the other. She opened her mouth to say something, shook her head and shut it. Then she opened her mouth again but closed it once more. Finally, after an exorbitantly long time she said, "You look great. Now, go catch some bad guys."

"Thank you. For a minute there I thought you might tell me that I wasn't up to snuff."

"I debated it, but you can't help that your hair is red. You also can't help the way that your nose sits on your face."

"Oh, okay. I'm not sure what that has to do with anything."

"Well, you would if you were a dog."

Before I could answer, the doorbell rang. "There's Rufus. Time to go."

CHAPTER 14

"Let's see what we can find out," Rufus said.

We were stationed outside the sporting goods store, hidden under a burned-out streetlamp. The lights were on in the shop, and I could clearly see the outline of a person as they walked around, more than likely closing up for the night.

"Do you think it's Jody?" I asked.

"I do. Drove by earlier and saw him inside."

"But now the blinds are pulled."

"Right. I'm sure it's still him, though."

I settled back in the seat and watched the man's outline move from one side of the store to the other. "So, what made you want to follow Jody first."

"Good question." Rufus ran his fingertips over the top of the steering wheel. "It was the way he acted the day of the altercation."

"How was that?"

"Not as worried as I thought he should have been."

"He seemed worried to me," I replied, recalling the look of concern on Jody's face.

"But he didn't act. He let me take the reins. He has magic, too. Otherwise he wouldn't have magical weaponry."

"That he can sell to whomever he chooses," I said, beginning to understand.

Rufus gave me a searching look. "Do you really think that a human can hold a weapon filled with magic and not feel anything?"

"I think it's highly unlikely."

"Me too. That's why he's on my radar."

"Well then, let's see what happens."

As soon as the words were out of my mouth, the front door opened and Jody appeared. He locked the bolt, pulled a metal barricade down and secured it to the sidewalk.

He walked to a sleek SUV and got in, fired up the vehicle and started down Main.

"Here we go," Rufus told me.

My heart pounded as Rufus fired up his own vehicle and we slid out of our spot.

"So, how are you going to make sure that Jody doesn't see us?"

"Easy. With this." He pulled an orb from his hand, whispered a few words and pressed it onto the dashboard. The entire inside of the SUV shimmered briefly before petering out. "That little bit of magic will cloak us from Jody. Other people, however, will be able to see us."

"Thank goodness. I'd hate for one of them to hit us because we were invisible."

"Exactly. That's why I made sure that he's the only one who's blind to us. Now. Settle back and let's see where we go."

I eased back onto the seat, even though I expected some sort of action to happen at any moment. I didn't know what, but I was waiting for something crazy to occur.

But as the lights from Main Street faded and the rows of houses turned to fallow cotton fields, I quickly started to realize that we were in for a drive, and a long one at that.

The cotton fields gave way to a lake with cabins alongside it, and it was at one of the cabins that Jody pulled in. Rufus slowed onto the road's shoulder and parked a couple of houses down, where we could still keep an eye on Jody.

He got out of his vehicle, went to the rear and pulled out what looked like a suitcase, and then headed up to the cabin, which had a slew of cars parked in the driveway.

Jody rang the doorbell and waited a moment, looking around as if making sure that no one was watching him. A few seconds later the door opened. I watched Jody shake someone's hand, and then he disappeared inside, suitcase and all.

"He's in," I said, suddenly breathless. My heart pounded and I couldn't shake the feeling that whatever we'd stumbled onto, it was big.

Rufus gave me a lopsided smile. "You ready?"

No. "Absolutely. Let's do this."

We exited the SUV and shut the doors quietly. The ground was littered with pine straw and cones, and every few seconds, I was stepping on a branch and grimacing as the crunch sounded from the bottom of my foot.

"Sorry," I whispered.

"It's okay," Rufus said. "No one's out here."

We finally reached the driveway, and I followed Rufus to the back of the house. It was built on a slope, with the front door level to the ground. Around back was the garage.

"There's probably a basement here where they're talking," Rufus told me.

We crept around to the back. It felt like every move I made, that something would happen—a branch would break, a glass would shatter, anything that would give us away.

No, there was no reason for glass to shatter. It wasn't a logical thought, but when fear sets in, logic goes out the window.

Rufus peeked into a set of windows on the opposite side of the garage doors. "Nothing," he whispered. "They must be on the first floor."

We picked our way up the side of the house until we reached the windows on the main level. I heard the murmur of voices.

"I can't make out what they're saying," I whispered.

Rufus blew into his hands, and a small fluttery insect-looking thing flew out from his palms.

"What's that?"

"That," he murmured, "is our key to hearing the conversation."

The little black dot of magic (which looked no bigger than a ladybug), squeezed through the window and made its way inside the house.

It picked up Jody's voice loud and clear. "Everything's going according to plan. Everything is selling great; we're picking up new customers every day."

"And the magic?" the other person asked.

Their voice was distorted as if it had been put through a machine. It was so warped that I couldn't tell if it was male or female.

"The magic," Jody explained, "is working beautifully. It's seeping into humans."

"Are they aware of it?"

"No, and I told the wizard Rufus that the magic had no effect on regular people. He bought it, but I thought he was going to catch me in a lie when a moment later that Stan went after Roy. The magic was already working on them."

"And what else?" the other person asked.

"Every weapon has been infused with your plan."

"Good."

It was really getting on my nerves that I couldn't see the person's face. I wanted to know who Jody was speaking to. This was clearly the person behind everything. This was the head clearer. Had to be.

I edged closer to the window. Jody sat in a chair in profile. The person he spoke to sat to his right, his chair facing away. Drat. Unless he or she got up, I'd never get a good look at them.

The mystery person spoke. "Our plan is working, then. Continue to infuse the message into it. We will turn the humans quickly that way. By the time the witching community gets wind of what we're doing, it'll be too late. The damage will be done."

Jody placed his ankle on the opposite knee. "Want to see what I've brought you?"

"Yes, please."

I held my breath as Jody leaned over and placed the suitcase atop his legs. He thumbed two locks, which snapped open. He lifted the lid, revealing a red velvet cushioned interior. Laying inside the case was a collection of knives—pocketknives to bowie knives that attached to a person's belt.

Jody swiveled the case around for the other person to see. "All of these have been infused with the magic of the next phase. The first phase, as you said, was to see how the magic affected humans. Now, in the second phase of the plan, we hone in that magic. Hold a knife and you'll see what I mean."

Jody handed him or her a knife and the person laughed. "Yes, I feel it. I see that all my problems are because of the wizarding community. I see that it's because of them that I don't have a job, that I can't pay my mortgage." The person laughed, a strange, distorted sound. "This is wonderful. But how will you ensure that when a witch or wizard comes in, that they don't touch one and discover what we're doing?"

"Easy," Jody said, "we swipe the magic off with a cloth for anyone with power. Let me show you." He took a blue fabric from his pocket and wiped it over the blade and then handed it back. "Now what do you see?"

"Nothing. I see nothing. Guthrie, you are a genius, the absolute right person to have put in charge of this project. You've outdone yourself. Now. I'm tired. It's taking a lot of power to keep those two unaware."

Those two unaware? What was he talking about?

"Of course." Jody snapped the case shut and rose. "I will let you have your rest."

Rufus gestured with his fingers, and the little bug floated up to the window. Jody must've seen a flicker of movement, for he glanced toward us.

Quick as a wink, Rufus and I darted to the sides of the window. My pulse pounded in my ears, and my heart thundered so hard I thought it might jump from my chest.

"What's that?"

"What's what?" the person asked.

"I thought that I saw something outside."

Rufus flickered a finger, gesturing for me to head off back down toward the garage. He motioned that he was going to walk in the opposite direction.

I wanted to shout, *Why don't we just use magic?* But we were dealing with at best, one wizard, and at the worst, one wizard and another magical being, both of which probably had a heck of a lot more magical training than I did.

"I'm going outside," Jody said.

"Go," Rufus whispered, and he was off, stalking quietly and quickly up the hill toward the front door.

As it was obvious that I couldn't just stand there and be caught, I made my way down the hill back toward the garage.

It may have seemed rude of Rufus, cruel even that he would have abandoned me, parting ways, but it made the most sense because first of all, the window that we stood at was tall, almost to the ground. Secondly, we'd been on both sides of it. So realistically, there was no way that I could have sneaked over to his side (or vice versa) without having been seen.

There was simply no other way.

As I made a path down the hill, I heard the front door open and stopped, my heart racing. Footsteps thudded on the porch. I was in the opposite direction, so I wasn't worried about being seen.

But I was worried about Rufus.

That was the direction he had gone.

"Who's out here?" Jody said loudly.

I pressed myself against the cabin, praying that he couldn't hear my heart.

I heard the distinct sound of a shotgun being loaded and locked. "I'm only going to ask one more time, who's out here?"

Please, please let Rufus get away. I wasn't worried about myself anymore. I was far enough away that I wouldn't be spotted.

"You're not going to get far because I'm going to find you," Jody called out.

His footsteps headed off toward Rufus's direction, and I scampered around to the driveway, keeping my back pressed flat against the cabin, doing everything that I could to be as quiet as a mouse.

I reached the top of the cabin and spotted a shadow in the trees. A yelp nearly escaped my lips, but Rufus stepped out. He pressed a finger to his mouth and reached for my hand.

Just as my hand slid into his, I heard Jody call out behind us, "I've got you!"

I turned toward Jody as he clicked on a flashlight. Rufus touched my shoulder, and I felt a wave of magic overtake me. I was falling fast through the woods. I saw his face but he was a mile away and Jody was approaching him with the shotgun. Then the portal closed, and I was at home.

And Rufus was back at the cabin, confronting Jody.

CHAPTER 15

I raced across the street to Willard's house and banged on the door. "It's an emergency! Please!"

A moment later the porch light snapped on and Willard stood in front of me, tying up his bathrobe. "Clem, what're you doing here?"

"It's Rufus. Something terrible has happened."

"Well, come in."

I swept past him, and Willard closed the door and then pointed to a chair. "Have a seat, Clem."

"I can't sit. I've got to stand."

"Okay, then stand. Can I get you some coffee? Water?"

"No, no. There's no time."

He folded his arms. "Tell me what happened."

So I did. I explained everything to him up until the point that Rufus sent me back and stayed there, at the cabin.

"Where is this place?" he asked, the most obvious question.

"I don't know," I said. "That's the problem. I might be able to get us out into the vicinity, but I'm not sure that I can get us exactly there."

He picked up his phone. "Can you try?"

"Of course."

"Good." He dialed a number and waited until a person answered on the other end. "Tuney? This is Willard Gandy. Yes, yes. I know it's late, but we've got a situation. A man may have been hurt up at the lake. I need you to come with me to stop the situation. Yes, at this time of night. No, it can't wait until the morning." He paused. "Because crime happens at all times of night, Tuney. Now, we'll come to your house, and then you can follow us out there. Okay? Thank you." He hung up and turned to me. "Tuney Sluggs is coming with. I'm going to quickly put on some clothes and then we'll head out."

"Okay." I managed a feeble smile. "Thank you, Willard."

He smiled grimly. "What else are grandfathers for?"

He quickly changed and we took his truck to Tuney Sluggs's home. Tuney had gotten out of his bathrobe and cowboy boots for once and was wearing actual clothing, which I was glad to see. The last thing we needed was to show up at a suspect's cabin with Tuney looking less than intimidating.

Not that the geriatric was intimidating to begin with, but I think you know what I meant.

Willard led the way out of town. The entire time my stomach was in knots. Would I remember the route? What had Jody done to Rufus? Was he okay? Oh no. What if they hurt him? I wouldn't be able to live with myself if that happened.

"Calm down, Clem," Willard said.

"I'm calm."

He glanced down to my fingers, which were twisted up in the hem of my T-shirt. "You sure about that?"

"Yes. No. I just want to get back there and make sure that Rufus is all right. I can't believe he did that, that he sent me away."

"I can," he said thoughtfully. "He wanted to keep you safe, and to make sure whoever else was there, that they didn't see you. He was not only doing you a favor, but he was doing the witches and wizards of this town a favor."

"How do you see that?"

"By making sure that you can spread the word about what you saw. You'll tell others, just like you told me."

"It was Jody at the new sporting goods store."

"Come again?"

"The man we'd been spying on. It was him."

Willard released a low whistle. "Why didn't you tell me that before?"

"I don't know. I guess that I was so worked up; I just wanted to keep things simple. He was there with someone else. So both of them are plotting to turn the humans against the witching population of Peachwood. Oh, turn left there."

Willard made the turn and glanced up into his rearview mirror. "Looks like old Sluggs is keeping up just fine."

"Good. We're going to need his presence at the cabin." If I could find my way back there. "In another minute you'll turn right."

Willard slowed the truck, and we made a right. As the vehicle raced along, the pastures gave way to the lake. We were on the right track!

Thank goodness. At least I'd done something right that night. We drove for a few more miles until I recognized the final road that we'd turned down.

"Turn there," I said. Willard did so and half a mile later, I spotted the cabin. "There it is! And there's Rufus's SUV."

His vehicle was still there, so we'd reached the right place. I could feel my pulse pounding in my ears. It was so loud that I could barely hear the nighttime insects and frogs chirping.

Willard parked in the driveway, and Tuney pulled in behind him. We got out and Tuney came over.

"So what's the story?" he asked me.

"Rufus Mayes was confronted by a man who was in that house, Jody, from Guthrie's, the new sporting goods store."

"I haven't had a chance to get in there and really browse. Is it nice?" he asked.

"Not the time, Tuney," Willard scolded. "Clem swears to have seen Jody put a shotgun to Rufus."

"Why was he doing that?" Tuney asked.

"Because we may or may not have been sneaking around trying to find out if he's up to something."

Tuney pushed up his hat and scratched his balding head. "Trespassing ain't good."

"I know. But there's Rufus's vehicle right there. He hasn't left. He was unarmed. If they did something to him, then that's illegal."

"Okay," he said, sounding reluctant. "Let's go check it out."

Tuney, Willard and I strode up to the front door. The police chief rang the bell, and I heard shuffling inside. Now the person who'd been sitting in that chair, the one I hadn't seen, would appear.

The door opened and out came a small woman who looked to be in her thirties. "Yes, officer?"

"Ma'am, I got a report that a man had a shotgun to another man in your front yard."

The woman's hand flew to her mouth. "What!"

A man, probably the woman's husband, appeared behind her. "What's all this about, Darla?"

"Tom, this officer says a man was wandering the yard with a shotgun."

Tuney glanced at me. "Was this the man?"

This was not Jody. "No, it wasn't him."

Tuney repeated to the man what he'd said to Darla. "We got reports about a man inside this house finding another man prowling about."

The man shook his head. "There's been nothing like that here."

"There's the man's car," I said, pointing to the road.

Darla and her husband glanced at one another in confusion. He spoke. "I'm sorry, but nothing like that happened here. We've had a quiet night. Got the kids to bed a little while ago.

Tuney looked at me and I could tell that he wanted to ditch the place, but I gave him the stink eye to end all stink eyes.

"Mind if I take a look inside?" Tuney asked.

The man nodded. "Not at all. Come on in."

I started to follow him, but Willard held me back. Once everyone had disappeared into the house, he said, "Tuney'll do his job, Clem. Don't you worry."

"I'm not worried." Total lie. "I know Rufus is here somewhere."

Maybe the man had been the one sitting in the chair and while Jody and the man spoke, Darla had been in the kitchen making cookies.

Right. As if that had been the situation.

Then I remembered what the unknown person had said, something about it was taking all his strength to keep the people unaware.

Oh my goodness. He'd magicked this couple and probably their children in order to meet Jody out here, where no one would suspect that they were up to anything nefarious.

My heart sank. Tuney wouldn't find anything. Of that, I was sure.

And when he returned to the door, Tuney didn't have hide nor hair of Rufus. He turned to the couple and tipped his hat. "Thank you for letting me in and sorry for the trouble."

"No problem, Officer," the man said. "Have a good night."

"Well?" I asked Sluggs as we walked back to our vehicles. "Did you see anything? Any sign that Jody was there?"

"Clem, I didn't see one thing. The inside of that house is clean as a whistle."

"Is it possible it's the wrong house?" Willard asked delicately.

"No, no. This was it. This was the house. Jody parked right here." I pointed to the now empty spot. "And there's Rufus's SUV." I turned around to look, but the vehicle was gone. "It's vanished. Look! It was there only a few minutes ago."

Tuney and Willard exchanged a look. "The truth is," Willard said, "I didn't see the vehicle. I saw a dark shadow that could have been made by the trees. But I didn't see Rufus's SUV."

But it had been right there. Hadn't it?

"Well, I'm gonna get some rest," Tuney said. "I suggest that you do the same, Clem. Wherever Rufus is, I'm sure he'll turn up in the morning, safe and sound."

"Safe and sound?" I repeated, unable to believe the words. "But he was taken. If he was safe, he would've called me by now. They've got him. You have to believe me."

Tuney came over and patted my shoulder. "What I believe is that you endured some kind of shock. It's okay. Trust me. I've seen it all in this business, and sometimes a good night's sleep will do a person wonders."

But I didn't want a good night's sleep. I wanted Rufus.

Willard clapped my shoulder gently. "Come on, Clem. There's nothing more that we can do here."

As we made our way back to his truck, I dialed Rufus's cell but it went straight to voice mail.

He was gone, taken. I knew it. And now I had to find him.

CHAPTER 16

I didn't sleep at all that night. I called Rufus's phone more times than I could count, hoping beyond hope that he would pick up the line. When he didn't, I left a message. There was no point in leaving more than one. He would get it, and if he could respond, he would.

Willard had driven me home and told me not to lose heart. I wasn't sure if he believed my story or not. He knew something had happened, but without any kind of real proof of *what*, there was nothing he could do.

When the sun brightened the windows the next morning, I felt like I'd been hit by a semi-truck. My head felt like it was swollen to the size of a beach ball, and my mouth was dry.

Of course I dialed Rufus first thing. Still no answer. In frustration, I screamed and tossed the phone on my bed.

"What's wrong?" Lady asked.

"Oh, my world is falling apart. That's all. No big deal."

"What happened?"

I explained everything and when I was done, Lady said, "Oh no, sugar. This is bad."

"Tell me something that I don't know."

"This is worse than bad."

"Once again, I'm well aware of that," I snapped.

"Well, don't shoot the messenger."

"Sorry." I sank onto my mattress. "I don't know what to do. It's all a mess. Tuney Sluggs didn't believe me, but I knew we had the right house. Where did Rufus go?"

"I don't know, girl. But I say we get out there today and start pounding the pavement. And call in reinforcements."

"What reinforcements?"

Lady narrowed her gaze. "The quilting bee kind."

I FOUND MALENE, Urleen and Norma Ray at their favorite quilting site —the Peachwood library.

Soon as I walked in, Malene opened her arms for a hug. "Oh, you look so beautiful. Why don't you come sit a spell?"

Lady's eyes widened. "Who is that?"

Urleen smirked. "This is how she's been ever since yesterday when she was blessed by Pastor Clark."

Malene gazed dreamily out the window. "Can't you just see all the colors out there? Don't you want to melt with them?"

"Sounds like someone's been smoking too much wacky tobacky," Norma Ray murmured.

"Oh, I would like some of that if you've got any," Malene said.

"She's all out," I said sternly. "Ladies, I have a problem."

"There are no problems here," Malene told me.

"You might not have any problems, old lady, but my girl Clem does," Lady said sharply. "Let her tell you all about it."

The whole time I talked, Malene sat with one hand under her chin, nodding and saying things like, "Mmm hmm," and "Is that so?" I got so tired of hearing it, I almost told her that I was about to *is that so* her. But I had a feeling she wouldn't get it.

When I finished, Malene said, "It'll all work out. Don't you fret, Clem."

I ignored her and turned to Urleen and Norma Ray. It was Urleen who spoke first. "I would be lying if I told you not to worry."

"Yes, I think we need to be very, very concerned," Norma Ray added.

My stomach twisted hard and I grimaced. "So what do we do? If I march up to Jody and confront him, he'll know that I know."

"And then he'll be after you." Urleen tapped her chin. "We've got to be stealth about this. The fact is, Rufus is missing, and we know who has him."

"We could follow him," Norma Ray said, "just like you did."

"He'll be on to that," Urleen told her. "He won't fall for the same trick twice. Jody will be on high alert."

"We need a way to get close to him and discover what's really going on," I mused.

Malene spoke. "What you need is a double agent. Someone who can infiltrate his network."

It wasn't a bad idea, but it was flawed. "How can we do that? He won't let a witch or wizard in."

A sly smile spread across Urleen's mouth. "Or will he?"

"I'm not following," I said.

Urleen pulled off her glasses and proceeded to wipe them with her shirttail. "What if we stage something that makes it very obvious that one of us hates witches or wizards. Something big. Something dramatic. Something that gets a lot of attention."

"Oh, I know," Norma Ray offered. "You mean something like two people battle in the square, and then one person wins and says all wizards are terrible."

"I was thinking something a little less dramatic but still effective," she confided.

That plan could work, but it had to look realistic and had to be executed to perfection. Ideas started to form, solid, ground-shaking ones.

"We have to strike the right balance," Urleen said, "between dramatic and honest."

"Where do we start?" Norma Ray asked.

A slow smile spread across Norma Ray's face. "Church. That's where we go."

Norma Ray and I exchanged a look. "What do you mean?" I asked.

Urleen slipped her glasses on and smiled. "What bigger platform could someone have in Peachwood than at First Baptist right now. It's the right place to make our move. The entire town will know about it."

"But there won't be church again for another week," Norma Ray argued.

Urleen shook her head. "Not with all the healing going on. Pastor Clark is holding service every night. He plans to heal the entire community."

Heal or destroy?

"Well then," I said, feeling a stir of excitement in my gut. "What are we waiting for? Let's get to planning."

$\sim$

"ARE YOU SURE ABOUT THIS?" Lady asked as we made our way inside the church.

"I'm sure," I told her.

I still hadn't heard from Rufus. At first I'd been deeply worried. But my worry had turned to anger. Now I was just furious. Whatever Jody had done to him, I wanted to do the same thing to him because there was no way that Rufus wouldn't have called or reached out to me. He would've let me know where he was so that I didn't worry. Which meant that whatever had happened to him, it was being done against his will.

And for that, I couldn't forgive Jody, and I considered him enemy number one.

Lady and I walked with a stream of people into the church. There were many folks I didn't recognize, who I guessed had come from neighboring towns to be healed. Pastor Clark certainly had some celebrity.

Lady noticed, too. "Looks like someone's famous."

She didn't say it so much as she was excited as she was jealous. In one day Pastor Clark had managed to steal all her thunder, which I supposed was a miracle in itself as the world knew that Lady could talk.

We passed a camera crew on our way to the entrance, and I overheard the reporter saying, "It appears that this pastor's celebrity has reached near and far. Even the talking dog has come to watch him perform his miracles."

Lady couldn't take it anymore. She whirled toward the camera and snapped, "I'm a miracle, too! I'm just as big a miracle as a man who can give people good attitudes." She lifted her nose and said, "Come on, Clem. Let's get inside."

When we got inside the sanctuary, it was nearly impossible to find a seat. The chamber was filling to capacity, and we still had fifteen minutes before Clark was supposed to start healing.

I spotted Norma Ray, and she waved me over. "I had to fight for these seats," she told me.

"Where's Urleen and Malene?"

"Up near the front somewhere." Norma Ray pulled an old-fashioned fan from her purse and waved it in front of her face. "We nearly talked Malene out of coming, but she insisted."

"Do you think she'll go along with the plan?" I asked.

"I sure do hope so. Otherwise, us even being here is moot."

"Norma Ray," cooed a voice.

We both glanced over to see Claire standing at the end of the row. "Oh, hello, Claire."

Claire smiled. "Hello, Norma Ray. Where's Malene tonight?"

"I think she's up front."

"Oh?" Her brow curled in delight. "Did she want to be close to the action now that she's been converted?"

"Converted?" I said, surprised by the term.

"Yes, converted to seeing all the good that Pastor Clark has done, and witnessing his miracles for herself."

"Oh, I thought you meant that her brain had been converted in weird way." Norma Ray turned to me. "Is that what you thought, too, Clem? That somehow Malene had been brainwashed?"

"Yes," I murmured, watching Claire carefully. There was something that I didn't quite like about her, as if she had a whole bunch of knowledge tucked away in her mind.

But Claire just laughed. "I didn't mean converted like that. I just meant what you saw yesterday morning, with her being changed is all."

"Claire!" Malene threaded her way through the crowd and came over, throwing her arms around the woman. "It is so good to see you. It's been too long."

Claire returned the hug. "It's only been since yesterday."

"I know, but it's just so wonderful to lay eyes on you. In fact, it's great to be alive."

Norma Ray rolled her eyes. "Here we go again."

"Are the clouds puffier and the sky bluer?" Malene said. "Or is it just me?"

Claire smiled widely. "Why, I would say that since Pastor Clark touched me, the entire world has become sharper and brighter. It's like before, I was just going through the motions, but now I'm truly alive."

"Me too," Malene agreed. "I've been introduced to a whole new world."

"I wish that she'd be *un*introduced to it," Norma Ray murmured.

"Well, I'd better get back to my seat," Malene told us. "Claire, would you like to join me?"

"I don't mind if I do."

As soon as they were gone, I said to Norma Ray, "What's going on? Why're you so frustrated with Malene?"

She exhaled a gusty sigh. "Ever since this whole thing started, she's been talking about how gorgeous the world is and how we need to be touched by Pastor Clark so that we can experience everything the way she does. Frankly it's getting on my nerves."

"Mine too," Lady agreed.

"You're not even around Malene all the time," I chastised.

"That don't mean I cain't relate."

Norma Ray shook her head. "Never mind. It's nothing that I need to complain about. You've got bigger things to worry about than me and my silly stuff. After all, we're here because of Rufus."

My heart twisted. "Yes, we are."

She patted my hand. "Don't worry, we'll find him. We'll discover where he's gone. He'll be okay, I have a feeling."

I prayed so. But what if he wasn't?

Stop. I couldn't do that to myself. I couldn't think the worst. I had to be positive. Being negative never got anybody anywhere.

Even if it did, that wasn't the route that I would take.

The lights started to dim, and Norma Ray whispered, "It's about to start."

"Oh, fancy lights," Lady said.

Loud rock music blared and people started clapping. The sanctuary went completely black, and when the lights came back up, Pastor Clark was standing in the middle of the stage.

He lifted his hands. "Who's ready to receive a miracle?"

The entire sanctuary burst into cheers.

It was time to hold on to my seat, because things were about to get real at First Baptist.

CHAPTER 17

Things moved quickly at the church. Pastor Clark called for anyone who wanted to experience a miracle, and up went a balding man who really, really needed new hair. It was life and death, he'd said. A blind woman was made to see, and a child who'd been stricken with an illness that paralyzed him from the waist down was gifted with the ability to walk.

The more I watched, the more I started to doubt that Pastor Clark was channeling God. It seemed more likely that he was a wizard and was manifesting this healing through his own magical abilities. The problem was, if he was using magic, how long would the healing last? Would it be forever, or was there a time limit on how long someone would remain well?

If there was a limit, it angered me because Clark was taking advantage of these good people, taking their trust and shoving it where the sun didn't shine.

"Who else needs a miracle?" Pastor Clark asked the crowd.

Urleen stood.

He spotted her and smiled. "What do you need done?"

"I don't need a miracle. I've got something to say."

The sanctuary was lit up again, and everyone could see Urleen as she stood near the front, her attention focused on Clark.

"What do you need to get off your chest?" he asked brightly. "Don't be shy now. You can say whatever the Lord is calling you to tell me."

I suspected that Clark thought Urleen was going to praise him or say that he was God's gift to creation. But that was not what came from her mouth.

"I have seen magic performed in my life. I have magic and the one thing that I'm never supposed to do is abuse my power."

"Okay," Clark said, looking confused.

"I have seen power be used for evil," she continued. "I've seen witches and wizards use magic for their own sakes, in the name of God. People in this very audience here, and it's disgusting. Using power for your own benefit is a horrible thing." She turned and glared into the crowd. "Those of you who've done this know who you are. You know what sins you've committed, and the Lord is coming for you. He is coming to seek his revenge, and you'll need to be ready. For when he casts his lightning rods of destruction on this earth, you will be the first to go."

"Amen," someone said.

Norma Ray shot me a worried look. I agreed. There was vitriol in the audience against witches and wizards, and it looked like Urleen was getting their anger warmed up.

She moved out of the pew and walked up to the stage like a woman possessed. "This town was once magical, and then we lost our magic because we're sinners. And now that we're getting it back, I've seen grave mistakes come from people. Folks using power for their own purposes. But for those of you selfish sinners, you will rue the day that you decided to use your magic for your own gains."

"Oh, okay." Clark looked a bit uncomfortable at having his spotlight stolen from him. "Was there anything else that you wanted to say?"

"Yes, there is more," she snapped. "This good man, this man of God, is doing the right thing. The power that he's been given is being used selflessly. He's helping us, all of us." She pointed her finger into the crowd accusingly. "The rest of you need to take heed and abide by his actions. For those of you who continue to walk the unrighteous path, you will know God's revenge, for it is coming. Just you wait and see! You will all bow down to the glory of God. You will witness the error of your ways. But I fear that it may be too late. Doom and destruction is coming for you all!"

There was a long silence as Urleen stared into the audience.

Then Malene shouted, "You go, girl! Speak your truth."

I had to stifle a giggle. But it was Pastor Clark who moved next, going over to Urleen and whispering in her ear. He patted her shoulder, and she took her seat back on the pew.

Norma Ray leaned over. "How do you think it went?"

"As well as can be expected, I suppose. She certainly got folks' attention."

"Do you think it was enough?"

As Pastor Clark started to speak, I watched the churchgoers lean over to one another and whisper. They were talking about Urleen. That, I was sure of. But whether they were saying good or bad things about her, I didn't know.

Yet there was one good thing about the entire scenario—folks were talking, and if they talked loud and long enough, it would spread around town about what Urleen had done.

I only hoped it spread to Jody and the sporting goods store by the next morning.

THE NEXT DAY I'd still not heard from Rufus. I went over to Malene's for breakfast and discovered her watching the local news.

"Look," she said when I entered. "Urleen's on."

Sure enough, someone had videoed Urleen speaking at last night's church service. I nibbled my finger as I watched Urleen pointing to the audience. The thing was, there wasn't any sound playing.

The newscaster said in voice-over, *"Last night in Peachwood, there was another service of healing and people being moved by the spirit."*

The clip cut off Urleen and on to Pastor Clark touching the blind woman's head. A moment later, she threw down her cane and proclaimed that she could see.

There wasn't mention of Urleen again. "Hmm. Do you think it's enough for our plan?"

"Of course it is," Malene told me. "Why wouldn't it be?"

"Because they didn't even air what Urleen said."

"You've got a point. But you've got to look on the bright side, Clem. Everything we're doing, it's going to put more focus on the next phase of the plan."

Right. The next phase. "But do you think we need something bigger? Something that will gain a bit more attention?"

Malene smiled. "Leave that to me."

Two hours later it was ten a.m. and we were standing down the street from Guthrie's. When I say *we*, I meant, Malene, Urleen and Norma Ray.

"Does everybody know their parts?" Norma Ray asked.

"I know mine," Malene said with a snort. "Look beautiful and do the best I can with this glorious life that I've been given."

Norma Ray pursed her lips. "Does everyone else know their parts?"

"Yes," Urleen replied. "And I'm ready."

"I'm ready, too," came a voice behind us. I glanced over my shoulder and spotted Jack lumbering up, staff in hand. He came up to me and placed both of his hands on his stick and spread his legs. "I heard about Rufus, kiddo. I'm sorry about it, but we'll find out the truth. They can't hide it from us forever."

I smiled and gave him a hug. "Thank you. That means a lot."

"You're very welcome." He turned to the women. "Now. What's the plan?" We filled him in quickly, and at the end of it, Jack nodded. "It's good. I like it, and it'll do all the right things. Get the right people's attention. But instead of Malene being the one throwing magic, I'll have a go."

I shot a quick glance to my grandmother, whose face was blank. "What? Why you?"

"Because anyone who knows y'all will realize that it's a ploy. I haven't been around town as long, so it's less likely that anyone will think I'm in on the plan."

"Malene?" I asked. "What do you say?"

She rubbed her chin and after a long moment replied, "It's such a glorious day, I can't see how we could go about it any other way."

One thing was for sure—whatever power Clark had worked on Malene, she was much easier to get along with. I kind of liked that about her.

"Then let's get to it," Urleen said. "Time's wasting."

"I'll go on up ahead and scout it out," Norma Ray said.

"Jack," I told him, "you're on."

Norma Ray peeked into the windows of the sporting goods store and gave a thumbs-up.

"Good luck," Malene told him.

Jack smiled and strolled down the street. He pointed to a pot of flowers that were sitting along Main Street (there were lots of pots for decoration). It rose into the air, and Jack let it hover there for a moment before he sent it crashing to the ground.

The crash was so loud and several people came out of their businesses to see what was going on. Jody, however, did not.

Norma Ray gestured for Jack to do the same thing again. This time he lifted a steel bench right out of the concrete and, with his magic, scrunched it like an aluminum can. The sound was so grating and horrific that people clapped their hands over their ears.

That was when Jody came outside.

Urleen, who'd been watching the whole thing, raced up. "I'm sick and tired of wizards and witches using their powers recklessly. You need to stop."

Jack turned to her and elicited a maniacal laugh. "I don't need to stop. You need to mind your own business."

He lifted another pot with magic and let it smash to the ground.

"I've had it," Urleen said. She pulled an orb from her pocket and threw it at him. He easily deflected it. She huffed. "I wish that every witch and wizard in this town who decided to use magic for evil would be stripped of their gifts! All of y'all need to be sent away. We need to do with you what they did to the witches in Salem—tag you and make you prisoners in your own home."

A few humans cheered her on. Oh. I hadn't hoped we'd receive that sort of response.

Jack pointed his staff at a light pole, and it started to bend, sending sparks of electricity crackling in the air.

"That's it," Urleen shouted. "I've had it!"

She threw another orb at him, and this time it engulfed Jack, staff and all. People cheered and she gave them a bashful smile.

Norma Ray turned to Jody. "Did you see that? She hates witches and wizards and wants them gone."

Jody tugged at the waist of his jeans, hiking them up like a man who wanted to look important. He walked down the street to Urleen and took her hand.

"You may have just saved several people from being harmed. You are a shining star in this town. I would like to offer my thanks."

Urleen smiled bashfully. "You would?"

"Yes. I'd like to reward you with something special."

"Oh, I don't need any thanks."

"Nonsense. If it hadn't been for you, some of the stores here in town might've been destroyed. Please. Come inside with me and I'll show you my appreciation."

"Well, if you insist."

"I do."

She followed him inside, and that was when Tuney Sluggs showed up. I raced toward him and waved him down. We couldn't let Jack get arrested, now could we?

"What's going on here, Clem?"

"You see Jack there? He was trying to fix something with magic, but he got tied up. I'll get him loose in a second." I paused. "So. Have you heard or seen anything about Rufus?"

"He still hasn't come back yet, huh?"

"He's been gone a day."

Tuney nodded. "Well, come by the station and file a missing person's report. In the meantime, fix that Jack fellow so that I'll stop getting calls about a nuisance."

"Will do." I tapped the lip of his door. "And thanks, Tuney."

He gave me a wan smile. "Sure, kid. Anytime."

As Tuney's police cruiser disappeared down the street, Urleen exited the sporting goods store. I caught up with her a little ways away.

"Well, did it work?" I asked.

She opened her purse and revealed the hilt of a knife. "It sure did."

CHAPTER 18

So we all went over to Willard's house to fill him in on
everything that had happened.

"So where's this knife?" Willard asked.

Urleen opened her handbag and revealed it. "Here it is."

Willard exhaled a low whistle. "Now that's a nice knife."

And it was. The hilt was made of polished wood and the guard
looked like silver instead of steel. The tip of the blade was sharpened
and glinted in the light.

"Touch it," Urleen told us. "You'll feel the power in it." No one
moved and she rolled her eyes. "Go on. It ain't gonna bite you."

"Of course it won't bite." Malene reached for it. "It's only a knif—
Oh! My! That's got a kick."

Everyone touched it then. When it was my turn, I curled my fingers
around the hilt and felt power stream into my hand. It was jolting and
sensuous. The knife seemed to whisper to me. It told me that the
witches were bad and that it could help me. It could give me what I
wanted.

When I released it a few seconds later, my fingers shook. "Wow.
That was no joke. Even if I like witches and wizards, this knife is going
to convince me otherwise. It's telling me that liking them is wrong."

Willard nodded. "It's a real problem. So. What do we do about it?"

"We burn down the sporting goods store," Norma Ray said eagerly. "That way, we'll get rid of the whole mess of weapons."

"But they'll just rebuild," I told her. "We need a plan that shuts the operation down permanently."

"Let's think," Jack said. "We'll come up with something."

While they were thinking, Willard said, "Any word from Rufus?"

"No, and I'm worried. Tuney Sluggs told me to come down and fill out a missing person's report."

He nodded soberly. "That's good. But I tell you what—we'll do one better."

"What's that?"

"We'll put up missing flyers, see if anyone's spotted him. Maybe we'll discover something that way."

"When do you want to do it?"

"How about right after this? I'll go with you to the police station, and then we'll put up the posters."

"Okay." He was kind to offer. "Thank you. I appreciate it."

"I think we should just take the knife and stroll right downtown and declare that we're not going anywhere," Malene said triumphantly. "That'll show them."

"I'm not sure who that'll show," Urleen said. "Let's come up with something else."

They thought and I tried, but there wasn't anything in me. My insides had been scooped out, tossed on the floor and with them, any hope that we'd come up with next steps. Earlier I'd had the energy to play this game, to work at this. But as the day dragged on and it was becoming more likely that something horrible had happened to Rufus, I simply wasn't able to focus. I didn't have it in me. All I wanted was to find him, to feel his strong arms around me.

I hadn't taken him for granted, but I simply assumed that Rufus would always be around to fix any problem. After all, whenever some magical dilemma reared its ugly head, he was the person who solved the issue. He came up with the plan; he had the skills to put things right.

For my entire life I'd been ignoring my abilities. Only recently had I started paying attention to them, and even then I still took a back seat to Rufus. Well, no more.

"I want a locator spell," I said bluntly.

Everyone stopped thinking and their gazes turned to me. "What did you say?" Malene asked.

"A locator spell, to find Rufus. We can make one, can't we? Doesn't such a thing exist?"

Malene, Norma Ray and Urleen all regarded one another. It was Norma Ray who spoke. "We haven't made something like that in a long, long time."

"But you can, right?"

Urleen nodded. "We can. But we need something of Rufus's. We can't create the spell without a personal affect."

"I'll get that." How, I didn't know. But I'd figure something out. "Can you do it?"

"We can do it," Malene said sharply. "And we'll need a compass orb."

"I don't know what that is," I said.

"I'll find one," Urleen told me. "We'll get that today, and then we can work the spell tomorrow."

"Tonight," I corrected. "Please."

Malene nodded. "Tonight."

What a relief. It felt like a burden had been heaved from my shoulders. My brain was suddenly working, and it churned, trying to come up with the next plan.

"I just can't think of anything," Norma Ray complained. "I'm not sure what we should do."

While we were all still pondering ideas, it was Jack who spoke. "We may not have to."

"Why's that?" Urleen asked.

He pointed to the knife. "Because I think it's trying to tell us something."

Sure enough, the blade glowed brightly. "What should we do?" I asked.

Jack reached down and grasped the hilt. A big laugh rumbled from his belly. "Oh, this is it! We've got them. Here." He handed the knife to Urleen. "See what it's doing."

She took and gasped. "Goodness."

"What?" Willard asked. "What's going on?"

Urleen was silent for a moment, and then her gaze slowly swept around the room. "There's going to be a meeting."

Malene patted her shoulder. "Looks like you're our point man for it."

"Well, then. We'd better get ready." Urleen rose. "Between now and then, we've got an awful lot to do."

~

IT DIDN'T TAKE LONG to make the report at the police station. I reminded Tuney Sluggs again that Jody from the gun shop had been the last person to see Rufus. He promised that he'd look into it. I didn't know if that was true or not, but I certainly hoped so.

When that was finished, Willard and I placed the missing posters up all around town. I hadn't had to do anything in terms of making the posters. Willard had done all that on his home computer, using a photo that he had of Rufus.

"Thank you for helping me," I said after taping a poster to a lamppost.

"You don't have to thank me, Clem. I'm worried about Rufus, too. I don't doubt that we were at the right house last night. I just don't know what happened between the time that you saw Jody there and when the married couple answered the door."

"You didn't recognize either of them? Know them from around town?" I said, following my grandfather down the street.

"Not at all. If they've used my pharmacy, it hasn't been in my presence."

"Maybe they use someplace like a big box store for their prescriptions."

"Maybe. But maybe they were also not who we thought."

I frowned. "What do you mean?"

"Could've just been a glamour."

"Look at you, using the magical lingo."

He smiled. "Yep. That's me. Using magical lingo everywhere I go."

"But you have a great point. Why hadn't I thought of that?"

"Because your brain has been focused on other things, like finding Rufus. You're somewhere between grieving and worried sick."

Gosh, he was right about that. I pressed a poster to the community bulletin board and pinned it in place. "I'm trying not to lose hope."

"I'm sure wherever Rufus is, he's giving one heck of a fight." Willard clapped a hand on my shoulder. "If I know him, he's not going down without one."

"I just wish that we had answers."

"You've got the locator spell coming up."

There was so much riding on it that I didn't even want to think about it. What if it didn't work? What if I couldn't get it to do what I needed? Worse, what if it *did* work and Rufus was…

Nope. I didn't need to go there. The best thing was to put one foot in front of the other and take life one moment at a time. Focus on one project before going to the next. That way I wouldn't drive myself crazy focusing on all the what-ifs.

"Do you know what thing of Rufus's that you're going to use for the spell?" Willard asked.

"I'll come up with something." What I didn't want to say was that I was going to break into Rufus's house and find something. I couldn't handle the disappointment in his eyes if I said my plan hinged around which window I thought would break the easiest. "I'm doing that next."

"You'll come up with just the right thing," Willard said, sounding like he had all the faith in the world in me. At least one of us did. "Let me know if I can be of any help."

"Sure thing."

Willard thumbed through his stack of signs. "Looks like we've got this area pretty well covered. Ready to hit some more spots?"

"Sure. Let's go."

WE SPENT two hours plastering missing signs just about everywhere we could, taping them to the doors of businesses (those who said it was okay, of course), and when we were just about done, Willard drove us back downtown.

"There's one more place that I want to visit."

"Where?"

"Follow me."

I got out of his truck and followed him into the sporting goods store. My heart pounded in my chest. This was a dead end. I knew it was. We would confront Jody, and he would tell us that he hadn't seen Rufus. He'd deny the whole thing, just like criminals always did.

"What are we doing?" I whispered to Willard.

"Just what you think we are." He stopped in the middle of the showroom floor and gazed around. "Which one is he?"

I pointed to the bald man behind the knives. "Him."

Willard strolled over. "Hey there. Nice place you got." He extended his hand. "Name's Willard Gandy. I run the pharmacy in town."

Jody returned the handshake all manly man. "Nice to meet another business owner."

"Same here."

Jody pointed to the knives. "So, what brings you in here today? Looking to buy a weapon?"

"No, not exactly. You see, I'm searching for someone." Willard placed a sign atop the glass case and slid it toward Jody. "I'm sure you recognize Rufus, as he was the man who stopped that terrible assault last week."

"I recognize him." Jody tapped the poster. "He's missing?"

"Ever since the other night, and I have it on good authority that you were the last person to see him."

Jody's face turned red; then he smiled quickly. "I'm not sure I know what you're talking about."

Willard leaned over. "I'm talking about a cabin in the woods, you showing knives to someone. You hearing something outside and then you finding Rufus."

"How'd you know about that?" Jody asked.

Willard didn't miss a beat. "Because Rufus called and told me so, right before he went missing."

"I'm not doing anything illegal, if that's what you're asking."

"I'm not," Willard assured him. "All I want is to find my friend. What you do on your time is your business."

My butt it was his business. Jody was working on taking all of the witching community down. He'd already done something to Rufus. This man was free game.

Malice flashed in Jody's eyes, and it sent a shiver straight to my core. There was no doubt that he was dangerous. Push him up against a wall and he would hit back, hard.

The emotion in his eyes was replaced with a warm smile. "I'm going to believe you, that you trust I'm on the up-and-up."

Right.

"And I'll tell you the truth about Rufus," he added.

My heart leaped into my throat. What truth? What did he know?

Jody smoothed his mustache. "Yes, I saw him."

And that was all he said. I wanted to shake him until his head fell off. But it was Willard who brought me back into the realm of sanity.

"Well," he said sternly, "where is he? You need to start talking and fast, before I call the police."

CHAPTER 19

$\mathcal{J}$ody took a deep breath, which made his cheeks ball like they were two pufferfish. "I don't know where he is," he confessed. "I found Rufus at the cabin and asked him why he was there. He told me that he was looking at some property in the area to buy. Of course, I didn't believe that, and I told him so. I said, look, I know we're on good terms. You did me a solid favor when you stopped that shooter in my shop, but right now you need to get out of here."

"Were you alone?" I blurted without even considering the ramifications of such a question. Why would I have asked it if I knew that Jody wasn't, in fact, alone?

"Yes, I was," he replied without missing a beat.

The last thing we needed was for Jody to suspect that we were on to him, so I didn't say anything else.

Willard took the lead. "What did Rufus do after you asked him to leave?"

"He left," Jody said. "End of story. I haven't seen him since."

He was lying. I just knew it but couldn't prove it.

Willard smiled and pushed the missing sign forward. "If you see Rufus or find out anything that could be of any help, let us know. Because no one's seen him since the night that you did."

"I'll keep an eye out."

"Thank you." Willard tapped the glass counter. "I appreciate your time."

"I thank you for coming in."

We left the shop, and as soon as we were far enough down the street that we couldn't be seen through the windows, Willard turned to me. "He's lying."

"Of course he is. But what can we do about it?"

"I'll call Tuney Sluggs and ask if he'll put some heat on Willard, if he'll press him about details, see if we can catch him in a fib."

I squeezed Willard's arm. "Thank you."

"That's what I'm here for." He rubbed his hands together. "I'm starving. What'd you say I make us the Willard special?"

"What's that?"

"It's two ground beef patties smothered in grilled onions and cheese."

My stomach hadn't rumbled in two days. I didn't have an appetite, but I couldn't tell Willard that. "Sounds great."

He took me to his pharmacy, which also had a soda fountain and a kitchen in the back. He made us some lunch, and we ate in silence. Neither one of us had much to say. There was too much weighing on us.

But that was about to change.

AFTER A LUNCH that I mostly picked at and scooted around my plate, I went home and collected Lady.

"Are my fans awaiting me?" she asked.

"Not unless they're at Rufus's house."

"I hate to break it to you, Clem, but my fans span the globe. They can be found in every nook and cranny in existence."

Somehow I managed not to roll my eyes. "Well, right now I need you to help me break into Rufus's house and get something personal of his."

"Why?"

"Because we're going to use it to locate him."

"Okay." She padded toward me, tail wagging. "I'm ready. Don't forget the golden hammer."

I'd just shouldered my bag and was about to walk outside. "What is it with you and that hammer?"

"I don't know. It just seems like a good thing to take with you when you know you might need to fix something or break into a place, or any other miscellaneous thing."

"Fine. I'll bring the hammer." I grabbed it from its spot in the closet. "But I didn't use it the last time you thought I was going to need it, so the same thing will probably happen again."

She shook her head. "You are such a doubting Clementine. Anyway, pick me up. I'm ready to roll."

I heaved her under my arm, and we left the house. Soon as we were outside, Lady glanced around.

"I don't see my fans."

"I think the miracles at the church have taken the place of a talking dog."

"Impossible. I'm one of a kind."

"So are the miracles."

She said nothing all the way to Rufus's house. When we arrived, the neighborhood was quiet. No one was outside working in their yard or walking down the street.

"Ain't that Rufus's SUV?" Lady asked.

Sure enough, parked out front sat the SUV. Hope rose in my chest. Maybe Rufus was back. Maybe he'd arrived and was taking a shower. Maybe he'd hit himself on the head and had a small lapse in memory, and he didn't remember me, but he'd managed to find his way home.

Chances were one to a million that was the case, but I could hope, couldn't I?

Feeling a surge of excitement, I took off for the house.

"Hey, I got short legs, remember?" Lady shouted.

Oh, yeah. "Sorry." I picked her up and took off. When I reached the front door, I banged hard on the wood—so hard that my fist ached. "Come on. Be home."

"Aren't you gonna be more angry if he is home than if he ain't?" Lady asked.

"Nonsense. I'll be relieved that he's alive."

Her ears lifted in alarm. "You don't think he's…dead, do you?"

I didn't answer, just pounded harder. "Rufus! Are you inside?" But after five minutes of pounding, I accepted that he was not there. "Well, it looks like we're back to square one."

"Square one? We haven't even found square zero," Lady said with a smirk.

I put her down and glanced around. "Do you see anyone outside watching us?"

"You mean watching us about to break into this here house?"

"That's the one."

"No, I don't."

Okay, the coast was clear. Now it was time for me to do…whatever it was that I was going to do. I stared at the door for a long moment trying to put together a plan. Windows flanked both sides of the door. I could just break one of those with my hammer and then get my hand through the hole and unlock the door. Or I could hit the doorknob with the hammer and maybe it would break. The problem with both of those ideas was that my hammer *fixed* things; it didn't break them.

"Why don't you just see if it's unlocked?" Lady suggested.

I took hold of the knob— "Right. Like Rufus would just leave his door unlo—" I pushed the door open. "Well, would you look at that? His door is unlocked."

"Works every time." Lady craned her neck right and left, scouting our surroundings. "Now get inside before someone spots us and calls the police."

"Excellent plan." I did as she said. As soon as we were standing in the foyer, I quietly shut the door behind us. "Okay, now to find the object that we need."

"Put me down so that I can walk about a bit. I'll be a better help that way."

I did as she said and absorbed the space. Light flowed in through the nine-foot-tall windows. Dust moats floated on sunbeams as they made their way delicately to the floor. The living room was formal with big velvet sofas and a statue from Greek antiquity. Wait. Was that a real Greek statue? Probably.

I careened past it and headed for Rufus's workroom.

"Wait for me," Lady cried. "I don't want to be by myself in here."

It was strange to be in Rufus's house without him. It felt like I was looking from the outside into the snow globe of his life. It felt wrong.

But I had to continue because Rufus needed me. So I kept on.

His wizard room was composed of big dusty tomes with cracking spines, jars filled with disgusting looking specimens that could be used in spells and of course, there was the cauldron with the three witches who wanted to eat my heart so that they could escape their jail. Good thing was, they didn't know that they needed to eat my heart, and I planned to keep things that way.

"Creepy," Lady murmured upon entering.

"It is creepy," I agreed. "But there's nothing personal here. Nothing that I could use for the locating spell."

"How about those pig's ears," Lady offered. "You think that's personal to him?"

I coughed into my hand. "Um. No. I don't believe so."

"Let's find his bedroom then." Lady pranced out of the room. "That's where we'll get the good stuff."

Wasn't that invading his space? There was something completely wrong about walking into his bedchamber—because Rufus was so formal that I couldn't even think of him referring to his private space as a bedroom. No, it would be a chamber—and poking through his things. It felt like an intrusion on his privacy.

"Maybe the kitchen will have something there," I suggested.

"What? The butter knife that he uses to smear jam on his toast every morning?" She glanced over her shoulder before placing her paw on the first staircase step. "You know that's not where we're gonna find the real deal. If we want to know Rufus, we've got to get to the heart of the man—and that's in his boudoir."

I rolled my eyes. She was right, of course. But I'd never been inside his room. What would I find?

I dragged my feet as I followed Lady upstairs. Twice she glanced over her shoulder at me as if trying to speed up my ascent. After a few steps I finally relented, making my way to the top.

"Which room is it?" I asked.

"I'll find it with my nose." Lady lifted her sniffer into the air. "It's over here."

She led me to a nondescript door that looked like any other. "You sure?" I said skeptically.

"That's it. His scent is the strongest here."

"Okay, then." I turned the knob, and the door swung open. I forced myself not to glance inside. "You first."

"Okay." She padded in nonchalantly. "Oh, Clem. You gotta see this for yourself."

Wondering what all the fuss was about, I stepped inside and sucked air. Walking in was like taking a trip to a museum. The room was long, at least as big as two chambers, with furniture sprinkled about—a desk on one side and a sitting area with two chairs and a table stuck between them on the other. A massive four-poster bed was pushed up against a wall, and it was flanked with two mahogany nightstands. Books were loaded onto one. I perused the titles—*A Tale of Two Cities, Anna Karenina, War and Peace.* You know, just some light reading before bedtime.

"He's got some knickknacks over here," Lady said.

I walked over to a curio cabinet that was tucked into one corner. Inside there sat a pair of antique glasses, an old flute and a few other books that were quite worn and slim—printings of Shakespeare's works.

"But there's nothing personal," I said. "Do all these things have the same meaning to Rufus? If so, I don't know what it is because he's never spoken about any of these things."

"What's that?" Lady said.

On top of his dresser, sitting all alone, lay a withered daisy with a red ribbon tied around the stem. I instantly recognized it. We'd gone spell hunting one afternoon, and I'd spotted the flower. Joking with him, I plucked it and handed it over as a gift. He'd gone even farther and magicked up the ribbon, which I'd wrapped around it, laughing the whole time at how silly it was to be giving him a flower.

He'd just smiled and took the present graciously. But I saw then that the gesture hadn't been silly at all—not to Rufus. That small token of affection (even though it had been done in a mocking way) had touched him deeply. In turn, it touched me that he'd been touched.

My fingers lightly brushed the petals. "This," I told Lady, "is what means something to Rufus. This is what we're going to take. But I've got to be careful with it."

I grabbed some tissue paper from a Kleenex box and wrapped the flower gently. Lady and I walked back downstairs, and first thing, she padded over to that statue.

"You think this thing is real?" she said mockingly, placing one paw on it.

The statue teetered. "Get back," I shouted.

Lady glanced up in fright and scampered as the statue came crashing to the floor, breaking into chunks. I raked my fingers down my face in frustration.

"Good thing we brought the hammer," she offered cheerfully.

I nodded. Yep, it had been a good thing after all.

CHAPTER 20

After fixing the statue, we left the house and managed to sneak away without anyone seeing us.

I called Urleen. "I've got the object that's important to Rufus."

"Great. Come on over. We're ready for you."

I drove out to Urleen's, which was located on the opposite side of town from where Malene and I lived. Her cottage was small, the color of buttercream, with robin's-egg blue trim and shutters.

When I knocked on the door, she answered. "Clem, come inside." She shut the door behind me. "Did you have any problems at Rufus's?"

"Not at all."

"The door was even unlocked," Lady told her. "It was like the house was expecting us."

"Not exactly," I corrected.

"Yes, exactly." She gave me a stink eye. "Man, am I starving. Urleen, you got any dog snacks or human snacks that may or may not taste like peanut butter?"

"I'm sure I've got something. Come to the kitchen."

She located a couple of dog biscuits from a cupboard and placed them in a bowl. Norma Ray and Malene were in the kitchen. Both women wore aprons and had yellow dishwashing gloves on their hands.

"I feel like I'm underdressed," I murmured.

122

"Oh, we'll get you an apron. Urleen's got a whole bunch of them," Norma Ray told me.

"I do a lot of cooking for the volunteer groups," Urleen explained as she handed me a lacy coverup. "Usually one or two of them is in the wash."

Malene smiled dreamily. "I'm just happy to be here."

Good grief. When was whatever Pastor Clark had done to Malene going to wear off?

I put on the apron and an extra pair of gloves that hindered my ability to grab things. "Okay. What do we do?"

Urleen took a spot at the head of the table. "Is everyone ready?"

"I'm ready. It's almost dinnertime and I'm starving." Norma Ray's tummy rumbled as if on cue. "Let's get going."

"I told you to have some crackers," Urleen said sourly.

Norma Ray withered under Urleen's stern gaze. "It's just not a very good snack."

"Beggars can't be choosers." Malene threaded her fingers and cracked her knuckles. "Now. Are we ready?"

"Yes." Urleen shot Norma Ray another dark look. "Let's begin."

She opened a mason jar and out fluttered three colorful orbs—one green for earth, a blue one that I instantly recognized as being connected to the water and a third white one that held the wind inside of it.

I immediately understood. The locator spell they were creating was using the three earth elements because if Rufus was somewhere on the earth, he would either be on the ground, in the sky or on the water.

It was an ingenious way to work the spell.

Urleen took the three orbs and began squishing them together while Malene and Norma Ray held hands. The work was tedious, and the spells didn't want to merge. But after a minute or two of kneading them like bread, they began to join.

When the colors had melded, Urleen opened her palm toward me. "The object?" I took the flower from my purse and carefully unwrapped it. Urleen pressed it into the very center of the orb. "Find Rufus, the man who holds this object dear. Search high and search low. Find him and return to us. Show us where he is. Do not stop until you have discovered his location."

Urleen stepped back, away from the table. This was it—the moment of truth. I exhaled a gusty sigh and waited for—what? The ball to take flight? For it to zip off and away?

I crossed my fingers, praying that this spell would work. The orb blinked on and off as if gathering energy. It rose into the air, and I squeezed my fists in anticipation. It then circled the room several times.

"That's what it does before leaving," Urleen said hopefully. "We've done everything right."

I held my breath as it zoomed around one more time.

"It's working," Norma Ray said triumphantly.

Malene fist-pumped the air. "We're the best spell hunters around!"

The orb headed toward an open window, blinked off and fell to the ground with a *plop*.

"That wasn't supposed to happen." Malene shuffled over and plucked it from the linoleum floor. She held it to her ear and shook it like a clock. "I think it's gone kerplunk."

"Let me see that." Urleen took the orb and cupped both hands around it. She grimaced and gave me a sad look. "I'm afraid Malene's right. It didn't work. I don't know why."

"We did everything correctly," Norma Ray insisted. "We didn't do one thing wrong. What could have happened?"

I remembered the golden hammer in my back pocket. I pulled it out and showed it to the women. "This is what happened. I fixed something back at Rufus's house that got broken, and this was the hammer's revenge. Whenever it fixes something, another thing breaks. This time, it was the spell that we desperately needed."

I wanted to scream. I wanted to toss the hammer into the ocean and let it get swallowed by a whale. I'd gone to all the trouble of stealing a flower that Rufus cherished and for what? Nothing. That was what.

"Can we do it again?" Norma Ray asked.

"We don't have more orbs," Urleen said. "This was all that we found, remember?"

"Oh, right. Phooey."

"And I don't have another personal thing for Rufus," I added, feeling deflated. "That was the best that I could find. His home is filled with stuff. But that, I know had real meaning."

"Oh, well. A tie would've worked, too," Malene said flippantly.

Wished I'd known that earlier.

"What do we do, then?" Norma Ray asked. "We've got to find Rufus."

"I think there's something else we have to do," Urleen told her.

"What's that?"

Urleen revealed the knife that Jody had given her. It was glowing an eerie lime green. "Get to the bottom of what's going on in this town."

~

URLEEN TOLD us that by holding the knife, she could sense where she was supposed to go.

"Where's that?" Norma Ray asked.

"Follow me in your car." Urleen grabbed her keys from a hook by the front door. "I'll take the lead."

"Shouldn't we all go in one vehicle?" Norma Ray asked.

"We can't." I shouldered my purse. "If we're seen together, then the jig is up."

Norma Ray grabbed her bag. "Okay, then. Y'all can ride with me."

"You go too slow," Malene complained.

Norma Ray smirked. "But I can't get into Clementine's truck, and your Miata is too small to fit all of us. So we'll have to take my vehicle."

Malene snatched the keys from Norma Ray's fingers. "I'll drive, then."

Norma Ray snatched them right back. "Oh no, you won't. I'm not getting arrested for letting you drive my car."

Urleen held the front door open and tapped her foot impatiently on the floor. "Come on. I don't have all day."

"Let's roll," Lady said.

So Malene, Lady and I piled into Norma Ray's Murano. Urleen took off down the street in her boat of a sedan, and Norma Ray followed behind...at five miles an hour.

Okay, maybe it was more like ten, but it wasn't fast at all. We were going so slow I wondered if we would wind up going back in time.

Needless to say, we lost Urleen about thirty seconds into following her. "Now where did she go?" Norma Ray said.

Malene glanced at me from the front seat. "I wonder."

"Let's drive around downtown and see if we can find her," I suggested.

"I'll just call her," Malene snapped. She pulled up Urleen's number on her cell and hit call. "She's not answering."

"Well, poop." Norma Ray took a right. "That would've solved a lot of things. But don't worry, we'll locate her."

We did eventually find Urleen's car. It was parked behind an old abandoned warehouse downtown.

"Oh, we've found her." Norma Ray did a little dance in her seat. "I knew we would."

Malene scanned the area. "Yes, good. Now hurry up and park so that we can get to spying, or whatever it is we're going to do."

Norma Ray parked about half a mile away so that no one would park near her and scratch the paint on the Murano.

When we got out, Malene stretched. "Isn't it a glorious evening?"

"Yes," I said tersely. "Let's get to spying. There isn't time to dillydally."

We headed over to the warehouse. The back door was unlocked. I placed a finger over my lips, suggesting that everyone be as quiet as church mice. Both Norma Ray and Malene made the same motion, and Lady closed her lips tight.

We were on.

The four of us sneaked into a hallway. Behind a big steel door it sounded like someone was talking. I opened the door as far as I dared and spotted many people, all sitting in chairs facing away from us. They were humming.

I glanced back at Norma Ray and Malene. I stepped out of the way and allowed them to see what I'd seen. They watched for a moment and then exchanged a confused look.

After a couple of minutes of people just sitting and humming, I motioned that we should step back outside.

When there, I spoke. "That's weird. What do y'all think they're doing?"

"Sounds like they might be in a trance," Malene said.

Norma Ray nodded. "I agree."

We'd have to ask Urleen more about it when she left the building.

"Ladies, I've been looking for you."

We glanced behind us and saw Jack coming up, staff and all.

"You've found us," Malene declared happily.

"I wanted to see how things were going with Rufus," he said to me.

I shook my head. "Not well. We haven't heard anything from him, and we tried to work a locator spell, but it didn't take."

"I'm sorry to hear that," he replied. "I've been on the lookout myself but haven't spotted him."

I patted his shoulder. "I appreciate you thinking of us. It means a lot."

I smiled up into Jack's warm eyes. He returned the smile, and I felt that he really did care about Rufus and wanted him to return. Emotion overcame me and I swallowed it down before tears spilled from my eyes.

"Well, ladies, what're y'all doing here?" he asked.

"Oh, we're spying on those people in that warehouse, there," Norma Ray told him.

Jack's brow quirked in question. "You're doing what, again?"

"The people in there are all humming as if they're in a trance," Norma Ray explained. "They got weapons from the new sporting goods store. You remember the big scene you made with Urleen, right?"

"Oh yeah, that's right."

Malene piped up, looking as if she hadn't liked being left out of the conversation. "Urleen's inside that building with all the others. She's humming away like them. We don't know what the heck's going on."

Jack rubbed his cheeks. "I think that I'd like to see that."

"We'll show you," Malene said. "Come on, ladies."

"I'll stay out here to make sure no one spots us," I said. "I'll whistle if you need to get out."

With that settled, they went inside to watch the chanting. I should have gone in, too, to figure out what was going on. But I just didn't have it in me. Rufus's disappearance was taking its toll. It felt like my will was being slowly drained away.

Dang it, Rufus! Why'd you have to send me back? You never should have done that. I would have stayed. I would have known what happened to him. I could have *helped.* He wouldn't have been alone out there, at that cabin. I wouldn't have Jody playing his mind tricks on me. I wouldn't have been doubting myself—like thinking that I saw Rufus's SUV when

Willard and I returned to the cabin, and then having it vanish only minutes later.

My sanity was slipping away. Is that what it felt like when you went insane? You thought one thing had happened, but it was really another?

I should have been inside helping my chipper grandmother and her friends. I wanted to seize this mystery by the horns, but I just couldn't. The fight wasn't in me anymore.

"Hello there."

I nearly jumped from my skin. I glanced over my shoulder and spotted Pastor Clark coming up. What was he doing here?

"You're Clementine, right?"

I forced a smile. One always had to smile around preachers. I'd been taught that as a child, and I wasn't about to drop my good manners anytime soon.

"Yes, I'm Clem. Nice to see you, Pastor."

He slid his hands in his pockets and joined me in front of the warehouse. Uh-oh. Did this constitute a moment when I needed to give the signal? Should I have whistled? *Calm down, Clem. Wait and see what he does.*

"I've seen you at a few of our gatherings," he told me. "What do you think?"

"Of the healing? It's a miracle. It seems to be. You gave my grandmother an entire attitude adjustment. I would absolutely call that a miracle. Nobody, and I mean nobody, has ever been able to get my grandmother in a good mood for more than about five minutes."

I said it as a joke, but the pastor didn't laugh. He looked off into the distance as if considering the shapes of the clouds as the sun set in the horizon.

"You know, it's amazing the work God does through me. Really amazing. I've been to so many towns and just happened to know Pastor Steve at the right time—when he was called away. Otherwise I never would've been able to bring all this healing to Peachwood. And Peachwood needs to heal, don't you think?"

The way he said it sent a chill down my spine. "What do *you* believe?"

His brow furrowed and he took an intimidating step forward. My heart jumped into my throat, but I told myself to be calm.

"I believe that this town has been under the rule of magic for a long time. Sure, it went through a dry spell, and you would've thought that the people then would've seen the error of their ways. They would have realized that turning to God was the path to take. But as soon as magic was reborn, what did the good citizens of Peachwood do?"

He paused for so long that I realized he wanted me to respond. After a moment I managed to squeak out, "I'm not sure. What did they do?"

He smiled bitterly. "When magic came alive again, the people, instead of rebuking it like they should have done, embraced it. They gave in to it with everything they had—all their fervor, their belief. Don't they realize that magic will be their destruction?"

Oh no. He was so very, very bad, and I was out here with him. Menace laced Pastor Clark's eyes. I was in danger. I needed to figure a way out of this conversation before things turned ugly.

But instead of saying goodbye, I wanted to challenge him, because I realized that Pastor Clark had been the man that Jody had shown the weapons to the night Rufus disappeared. Clark was the mastermind behind the clearers that had come for us. I was at war with Pastor Clark, whether he knew it or not.

"Magic is what one does with it," I bit back. "It can be used for good. It can be used for evil. But silencing those who wield it never works."

He smirked. "You don't think so?"

"No."

Pastor Clark nodded. "Things are about to change here in Peachwood. I'm afraid those of you who have magic are about to see just how much."

"And I will fight you with everything I've got. You wear the mask of God on your face, but you're really hiding behind the face of the devil."

He gasped. "I am a servant of God."

"God does not demand destruction."

"Mine does," he spat.

We stared at one another and silently knew this was war. One of us would win, and one of us would lose.

"Where's Rufus?" I demanded.

His eyes narrowed. Before he could answer, Malene, Norma Ray and Jack exited the building. Malene spotted Pastor Clark and sidled up to him.

"Clark, it's so good to—"

I yanked her away (softly, for she was old and doughy). "He's in on it. Pastor Clark is behind this whole thing. He wants magic gone. He wants *us* gone."

Malene and Norma Ray gasped. It was Malene who spoke. "Is that true, Clark?"

He nodded. "Let's just say that a battle is brewing, a battle for right and wrong. The side of God will win, and the rest of you will lose. Now, good night."

Without another word, he slipped inside the warehouse, leaving us alone in the empty parking lot.

CHAPTER 21

I was shaking by the time we returned to Malene's house. Jack had left to get Willard, leaving Lady, Norma Ray and myself. Malene brewed coffee while Norma Ray prattled on.

"He seemed like such a nice fellow. How could Pastor Clark turn on us like that?"

"He never turned on us," I explained. "He was against us from the very beginning. Argh. My instincts in the beginning were right. I knew there was something off about him, and I should have pushed for it. If I had, maybe Rufus would be here now."

Norma Ray shushed me. "You can't blame yourself for that. His disappearance wasn't your fault."

Then why did it feel like it was? That I should have *not* done what he told me but chased after him, followed him and stuck together? But even if I had, there was no guarantee that he wouldn't have sent me through a portal again. Probably the same thing would've occurred, just at a different place and at a different time.

"Norma Ray's right." Lady pressed her nose to my leg. "You cain't blame yourself, Clem. Besides, we should've known something was up when Pastor Clark stole all my thunder. Me talking should've been the biggest story on Sunday, not him healing people."

"So is he using magic?" Malene asked, entering the room with a tray stacked with a pot of coffee, cups and cookies.

I took it from her and placed it on the living room table. "He has to be, right? Using magic and not God's power."

Norma Ray thanked Malene for a cup of coffee and bit into a chocolate chip cookie. "He must be wielding magic. But that's not what the town believes."

"Or the news, for that matter."

I took the cup that Malene handed me and sipped it. The brew was strong. I was glad for it, as I was sure the caffeine would be exactly what I needed this night. We had a lot of work to do and were starting at ground zero.

"We have to expose him," I murmured between bites of cookies. "That's the first thing that must happen."

"But what about the humming?" Norma Ray asked. "When Malene and I went back in with Jack, it was obvious those people were in a trance."

I'd known as much, but to have Norma Ray confirm it was unsettling. "Has anyone heard from Urleen?"

"No," both women said in unison.

"We need to make sure she's okay."

"I'll call her." Malene picked up her phone and dialed. It must've gone straight to voice mail, for she said, "Urleen, it's me. Give me a call when you get this."

"She's probably still humming," Norma Ray mused.

"Probably." Malene placed the phone on a table and sat on the couch. "They could be there all night."

"We shouldn't have left her," I said, frustrated.

Malene gave me a sympathetic look. "All of us wanted to leave after our encounter with Clark. Besides, there wasn't anything that we could do. We don't know what sort of power those knives hold. What if we'd marched into that warehouse and were attacked by those people?"

She had a point. But that didn't make me feel any better.

"Malene's right," Norma Ray said. "We did exactly what we needed to. Don't beat yourself up about that."

"Where do we go from here?" I asked no one in particular.

"What we need to do," Lady said smartly, "is to get into that church and prove that Clark's a phony."

"But how're we going to do that?" I said.

The door opened and Willard entered, followed by Jack. My grandfather greeted everyone and took the coffee and cookie that Malene offered. Jack did the same.

Then both men settled down, and we caught Willard up to speed.

"So it's Clark, is it? I knew something was fishy about him. Anyone who claims to work miracles is usually lying."

"We've got a lot of people against us," Jack said. "And no Rufus to help fight."

My stomach knotted but I pushed the angst aside. "We were discussing revealing Clark's identity to the congregation, in front of everyone, when he's working one of his 'miracles,'" I said, using finger quotes over the word. "But we hadn't gotten into specifics."

Jack wiped cookie crumbs from his beard. "We know he's using magic."

"Right," I said. "That's one of the calling cards of the clearers. Use of magic."

"Then why don't we just block it?" Norma Ray suggested.

We all exchanged a look, and then Malene focused her attention on Norma Ray. "What do you mean?"

"Block his magic." She shrugged as if it was the easiest thing in the world. "Surely he's using some type of glamour to do all that healing."

Malene frowned. "It doesn't feel like a glamour."

"But it must be," Jack said. "It makes the most sense. If it was healing power that Clark is using, he would've overdrawn by now."

Now I was confused. "What do you mean?"

Jack brushed cookie crumbs from his fingers. "Let me put it this way—I once witnessed a great healer witch draw a tumor from a person. Doing so cost a great toll on her. She had to lie in bed for two days after performing that much healing."

"Perhaps Clark has been working up his stamina for years," Willard suggested.

"That's possible, but I doubt it," Jack mused. "What these people want is to create a big spectacle. They want fireworks and for it all to happen fast, so that they can get their desired outcome, which we know to be the destruction of the witching community in this town. The best and fastest way to do so is to pull a con on the good folks of Peachwood."

"Oh, I get it," Lady said. "Let Clark do all the fancy healing while the gun guy does the real work."

"Bingo." Jack clapped his hands. "While everyone's distracted talking about what's going on at the church, the gun shop guy is building an army."

Norma Ray gasped. "You think so?"

"Why else would all those folks have been hypnotized in that room?"

I shot Malene a worried look and she grimaced. We were thinking about Urleen and what had happened to her. What *had* happened to our friend?

"Maybe you should call Urleen back," Norma Ray said, seeming to read our minds.

Malene did so, and this time she reached her. "Where are you? We're at my house. I've got coffee and cookies. You're coming? Okay, we'll be here." She hung up. "Urleen should arrive in a few minutes."

"Why didn't she answer before?" Norma Ray asked.

Malene shrugged. "She must've still been in the warehouse." She glanced at Jack and Willard. "Should we be concerned about her? What if she's one of them? What if she's turned?"

Lady piped up all dramatically. "What if it's like in that movie, *Invasion of the Body Snatchers*? What if her body's been swapped with an alien's? I haven't seen any weird flowers about town, but what if they brought them into the warehouse and passed them out after we left?"

"You're making me itch just talking about that." I scratched my shoulder. "Please don't discuss things like that. It's not possible."

She cocked a brow at me. "How do you know, Clementine? How can you be sure?"

"Lady's right," Willard said. "From what you've told me, it seems like something sinister could've happened to Urleen in there. We need to be ready for when she arrives."

"What should we do?" Lady asked. "Do y'all want me to attack her ankles? Bite them until she howls?"

"Hold on there, Rover," I said. "Let's be reasonable. We'll talk to Urleen and then make a move if we need to."

Everyone agreed and then we waited in silence. The tension was as thick as a slice of bread off a good French loaf. Maybe even thicker.

By the time Urleen rolled up, I knew she'd be suspicious of how quiet we were, so I said, "Find something to talk about. Right now."

As Malene moved to answer the doorbell, Norma Ray said, "So I've been trying that Beano after certain meals, and do y'all know what? It really works. There will be no gas."

That was not the sort of conversation that I'd had in mind. But whatever floated her boat.

Urleen entered looking completely normal. Her hair was in place, and her clothes were pressed. There was nothing unseemly about her. Lady approached cautiously and gave a sniff, then looked at me and nodded, giving her seal of approval.

Urleen noticed and I wanted to slap my face. "Is everything all right?"

We gave a chorus of, "oh, yes," "absolutely," "never better," before Urleen took the coffee that Malene offered and sat.

We did a collective inhale, watching for any sign that Urleen was not herself.

"So what took you so long to get here?" Norma Ray asked.

"We were in that room, and the humming, it was terrible." Urleen swatted the air. "I never thought I'd get out of there."

"All that humming," Malene said, "did it make you feel different?"

"Different? How?"

My grandmother nibbled the edge of a cookie. "I don't know, like maybe you wanted to take up arms against the good witches and wizards of Peachwood?"

Urleen gasped. "Malene, what has gotten into you? I'm working undercover. I'm not going to turn on my friends."

"So you say. Tie her up, fellas."

Willard and Jack exchanged a confused look. "Um, Malene," Willard said.

"What is it?" Malene pointed a cookie at Urleen like it was a dangerous weapon. "Get her hog-tied! Hurry! Before she turns on us."

"Malene," Willard repeated gently, "I don't think Urleen has any plans to turn against us."

"You don't know that. She was gone an awfully long time. She was humming along with the rest of them. Whatever mind control Clark and Jody are up to, she's part of it."

Urleen shook her head. "Malene, I hope you're joking. I'm the same old Urleen. Nothing's changed about me. Besides, I had these in my ears." She pulled out a pair of earplugs from her purse and showed them. "I'm safe. Now, listen. Do you want to find out what I learned?"

"Yes," Jack said eagerly. "Tell us."

"Okay," Urleen started as Malene approached her slowly, the cookie still in her hand. "Um, Malene, are you going to put that down?"

"The only thing standing between you and me is this here cookie, and I plan to keep things that way."

"Suit yourself," Urleen replied, eyeing the cookie skeptically. "What I discovered is that the pull of the weapon I have is stronger than I ever considered."

"What do you mean?" I asked.

"The images that it put into my mind—that I needed to take my weapon and rise up against my own kind—well, let's just say that it's powerful."

"How powerful?" Malene demanded.

"Very," Urleen admitted. "When I was in the room humming, I could feel the entire space shift, like I was part of something, as if we were a flock of sheep and if one of us jumped off a cliff, I would jump as well."

"Well, I'm glad you didn't," I said.

"Me too, but I was fighting it," she explained. "The other people in that room, there wouldn't be any reason for them to fight against the power."

"Maybe," Willard said. "Maybe not. Perhaps they've got friends and loved ones who are magical."

"I think you'd need more than that," Urleen said quietly, "in order to fight the strength of that spell."

It was time to cut to the chase. Yeah, yeah, it would be impossible for someone not to succumb to the spell, but that wasn't the most important information to glean from her experience.

"When are people going to act?" I asked. "When will the uprising occur?"

Because an uprising it would be, surely. Urleen glanced at the floor in thought. When she glanced back at us, her eyes glowed green, the same lime color as the knife. "It's starting right now."

CHAPTER 22

I jumped from my seat and grabbed the closest weapon, which was an empty paper plate. "Stay back! You won't take us alive!"

Urleen's lips pulled back into a sneer, and Malene lurched forward with the cookie. "I knew something funny was going on! Take that!"

She threw the cookie and hit Urleen in the shoulder. The color in her eyes blinked before fading out. "What are you doing, Malene? Clem? I was just kidding."

"I was about to bite your ankles. So if you were kidding, you did too good a job at it," Lady barked.

Urleen grabbed her sides and laughed. "You should've seen your faces. I just used a small orb spell that I had in my pocket." She wiped tears from her eyes and pulled a deflated green orb from her pocket. "Wow, I got y'all good."

"There are times for games, and that was not one of those," Norma Ray said with a sniff. "We don't appreciate being joked with."

Jack chuckled. "I disagree. It was exactly what we needed to break the tension. Sometimes you need a good old-fashioned laugh to crack open a sobering moment."

"That's what I was thinking," Urleen said, wiping tears from her eyes. "But back to what you were asking—*when* will something happen?

I don't know. But I sense it's soon. I think they wanted to see tonight maybe how many of us there were, to see if the clearers had enough of an army to make a difference in this town."

"Because it's a numbers game," I added.

"Exactly." Urleen wiped her eyes with a tissue and sat back down. "As long as they have enough people, then they'll act."

"Malene," Willard said, "how many folks would you say were there tonight?"

"Probably two hundred or so."

"Yep," Norma Ray agreed. "That sounds about right."

Willard gave Jack an appraising look. "Are you thinking what I'm thinking?"

"That Operation Clear Peachwood is about to be a go?"

Willard nodded. "That's the one."

"I sure am." Jack turned to us. "Ladies, we all need to be on high alert, because any day now this town is about to change, and not in a good way."

I TOSSED and turned that night, dreaming of people walking down my street with pitchforks. I ran out to stop them, but the people, my very neighbors, turned on me with their weapons and chased me into my house, trapping me inside. They broke windows and got in, finding me hiding in my closet. As their hands closed around my arms and legs, I woke up, heart racing, breath coming fast.

It was morning. Daylight streamed through the blinds. It was time to get up and face whatever it was the day had to offer. I went about things slowly, missing Rufus so much that my heart ached. I'd spent part of my life hating him and now that I loved him, I didn't want him gone. I wanted him there every day. I wanted to chat with him first thing in the morning, hear his voice right before I went to bed. I missed him so much that my entire body throbbed with misery.

I opened my fridge to eat something, but I didn't have any appetite. I didn't even have the motivation to make coffee.

"Cheer up, Clem, we'll find him," Lady said.

But it had been days and Tuney Sluggs hadn't called. Had I done enough? I'd gone back to the cabin right after Rufus had sent me away. I'd filed a missing person's report. Willard and I had gone to the sporting goods store to talk to Jody. Yes, he was lying. He knew more than he was saying, but I didn't have proof of anything.

My phone rang. I didn't recognize the number, but it looked legit and not from a telemarketer, so I answered.

"Hello?"

"Clem? This is Trina, from Bender's."

Wow. With everything that was going on, I'd almost forgotten about Trina. "Hey, what's up?"

"You posted those signs about Rufus, right? The ones that say he's missing."

My blood pooled at my feet. "Yes, I did."

"Well," she paused, "I think that I saw him—yesterday."

"Where?"

"I don't want to say over the phone. But can you come here, to Bender's?"

I was already pulling on jeans. Forget showering. This was more important. "You're there, now?"

"Yes, I'm here."

"I'll be there in five minutes." I hung up and pulled on a mostly clean T-shirt that lay crumpled at the foot of my bed. "Lady, I'm heading out."

She appeared in my doorway munching a bite of food. "Where're ya going?"

"Trina from Bender's thinks she saw Rufus, but she didn't want to explain over the phone."

"I'll come."

"You need to finish your breakfast."

"Get me a paper bag, woman. I'll eat on the way."

We arrived downtown a few minutes later. I was about to park when I noticed that a crowd of people had formed in front of the building.

"Is the line that long?" I murmured.

"I don't think so," Lady said. "Look."

I slowed and saw that the people were pounding on the glass. "What's going on?"

"Hurry up and park so that we can find out."

I did as she said, and we got out. As I approached the crowd, it was obvious these folks weren't doing any kind of friendly tapping on the windows. They were beating, hard.

"Let us in," a woman shouted.

"We want the witch," a man added. "She's been poisoning our drinks."

Oh no. They'd discovered that Trina had special talents when it came to making drinks, and they were ticked.

"Some of these people are the ones from last night," Lady told me, "from the warehouse."

I spotted Julie and Trina inside the shop, alone, huddled in the back. The fear on Julie's face hurt my heart. Surely Tuney Sluggs and his police officers were on the way, but what if they didn't reach the store before the crowd broke in?

Was this part of Clark's plan or just a random stroke of luck? "Come on, let's go around back and see if we can get Julie out."

We raced to the back, but there were people guarding that door, too. A man shouted, "You're going to pay for what you did to my wife—made her happy."

I nearly rolled my eyes. Right. Because happiness was a crime.

But the bigger problem was that I couldn't get Julie and Trina out, and the banging from the front was getting louder. When I took Lady back around to Main Street, people were hitting the glass harder. They were going to shatter it and storm the place.

Julie and Trina would be hurt.

We had to do something.

"Put me down," Lady said.

"I'm not—"

She squirmed and practically jumped from my arms, so I did as she said. "Lady, what are you doing?"

"Listen here, y'all scallywags! You ain't got no right to hurt that woman. She ain't the only one with magic. I've got magic, too."

Very slowly Lady's voice filtered above the melee, and people began to turn in her direction.

"Do you people even know what you're doing? My boss here, Clem, she drank one of Trina's coffees and so what, she might've almost stripped naked and ran down Main Street, but she wasn't hurt by it."

"Is that a talking dog?" a man asked.

"Yes, I'm a talking dog, and I'm full of magic! I'm so full of magic that I can burn the hair right off the top of your head with one fireball!"

A woman shrieked. "Please, don't hurt us!"

Lady puffed up her tiny chest. "I will hurt y'all! I will make you pay with blood, sweat and tears if you don't leave those women alone."

A man turned toward Lady, a cold sneer on his face. "What say that instead of getting those women, we get you, little dog, and teach that witch what we do to magical beings?"

Lady backed up until she bumped into my leg. "That's not exactly part of the plan. Y'all need to be settling down, now. Don't be coming after me—unless you want your hair on fire," she said meanly.

But they weren't taking the bait. "If you could work magic, little dog, you would've already done so," the same man said.

"That there dog is an abomination," a woman shouted.

"Let's rip it limb from limb," another man declared.

"Clem," Lady yelled.

I scooped her into my arms as the crowd approached. Well, Lady had accomplished her main goal—distract the mob and get them to stop focusing on Bender's. The only problem was that now they wanted to kill us—or her, at least.

What to do? I had some magic in me because I was always naturally charged, but I couldn't work it on a crowd this big. I couldn't stop them all. Oh no. What would Rufus have done? Why wasn't he here?

A man with pure malice in his eyes lunged for Lady just as the morning exploded.

A woman gasped. Everyone became motionless. I jerked around and saw Tuney Sluggs standing in the middle of the street holding his revolver to the sky. Smoke bloomed from the barrel.

"Just what in the world do y'all think you're doing?" he asked.

The people who had all been ready to eat Trina's heart for breakfast balked. "Well, nothing, sir," the man who'd led the melee sputtered. "Absolutely not one thing."

"Right," Tuney said with a heavy dose of sarcasm. "Doesn't look like nothing when I get calls about you pounding on the windows and about to attack a tiny dog."

"A talking one at that," Lady said.

Tuney glanced at her quizzically and then opened his mouth to say something and stopped. Started again. "Y'all get on home. If I see one of you anywhere near this coffee shop, I'll haul your butt to jail."

"Yes, sir," folks said as they hung their heads and shuffled away.

Once the crowd was cleared, Tuney approached me. "Clem, I'm sorry to say, but I haven't got any leads on Rufus. Haven't heard a thing or talked to anyone who knows anything."

"I know. It's okay." I was tempted to tell him that I was there because Trina had sworn she'd seen Rufus, but then Tuney would probably tell me to stay out of it as we were dealing with an official missing persons case. "Something will come up."

"Yes, it will," Tuney said. He told me goodbye and left.

I hauled butt to the shop. Julie unlocked the door as I approached. "Oh my gosh, Clem. That was just awful."

"What happened?"

She let me in, gazed around and locked the door once more. "Just to be safe. I know Tuney took the steam out of some of those people, but more could be coming."

"This is all my fault," Trina admitted. "I just don't know my own magic. I don't plan on putting magic into the drinks I'm making, but it just flows out of me, into the cups and then...well, you see what happens."

I took her by the shoulders. "You didn't do anything wrong. You make a cup of coffee that makes people happy. Why, last time I was in here, people were gushing about how wonderful of a job you were doing. They need your drinks, Trina. You should accept that."

She shrugged, clearly not convinced. I wasn't sure how much more sunshine I could blow up her butt, though. There were other things to discuss.

"You said that you saw Rufus?"

Trina nodded. "Yep. Last night."

My chest tightened to bursting. "Tell me everything."

CHAPTER 23

"Have a slice of coffee cake," Julie told me.

She'd made each of us a cup, and the three of us had sat at a table. Julie also brought over a beautiful round cake with a crust of baked sugar on top.

She sliced a knife through it. "Fresh from the oven this morning."

Though my general rule was chocolate for breakfast, I wasn't about to look a gift horse in the mouth. "Thank you."

Once we each had a thick piece of cake sitting on a plate before us, Julie turned to Trina. "Tell Clem what you saw."

"It was Julie who convinced me to call you," she admitted. "At first I hadn't wanted to, but we talked about it"—the two women shared a look—"and she said that it was best if you knew everything."

Oh goodness. This sounded terrible. As if to confirm that, Lady pressed her body to my leg. Of course, that could also have been because she was looking to catch a crumb of cake that fell from my mouth.

"What happened?" I asked.

"Well," she said slowly, and Julie nodded. It was only then that Trina continued. "I saw Rufus last night."

"You're sure?"

She nodded. "I'd met him before. I'd seen him with you, and there was no mistaking him."

My heart leaped into my throat. This was amazing news. Rufus was okay! He was nearby. I could find him. It took all my will not to grab Trina by the arms and shake the rest of the information from her.

"Where was he?"

"Do you know that old warehouse in town? The one that's only a few blocks from here?"

It was the same place where everyone had convened at last night. "Yes, I do."

"Well, I saw him. It was late and I was out taking my dog for a walk. I spotted him walking out of the building. He was with someone. I think it was the guy who owns the new sporting goods store."

"Jody?"

She nodded. "That's the one. They came out together and I know it was Rufus because he turned toward me and I saw his face clearly. But Clem, he wasn't himself. He wasn't the same person that I'd seen before."

"What do you mean?"

Her voice trembled. "His eyes, they glowed green."

Oh. My. Gosh. What did that even mean? Urleen's had glowed but she said that she was only playing a prank on us. Had she been lying?

"And it wasn't just a regular green," Trina clarified. "It was lime green."

It couldn't have been a coincidence. Rufus had been put under the same spell that half of the town would soon be succumbing to—if Jody and Clark got their way.

Lady tipped back her head, met my gaze. "What did I tell you—*Invasion of the Body Snatchers*."

Looked like for once my dog was right.

I suspected that tonight would be the night when Clark would act. He couldn't risk Rufus being seen around town too much, because that would raise questions like, why was a missing person, who'd be completely happy in his life, avoiding returning to his house, his friends?

Yep. We needed to be ready and beat Clark to the punch.

I called an emergency meeting right after leaving Bender's. "Malene," I said, "round everybody up. We've got a town to take back."

We met at her house a few minutes later. Willard was trying to track down Jack, but Urleen and Norma Ray were in attendance while Malene put out finger sandwiches filled with pimiento cheese spread.

Since I was still full, I passed on eating, but Norma Ray was gobbling them down like they were going out of style. "These are so good, and I skipped breakfast because I'm trying to lose weight."

"Well, you'll *gain* weight if you keep eating like that," Urleen told her.

She stuck her tongue out at Urleen.

"Okay, everyone," I said, "Jack and Willard will just have to catch up because we've had a Rufus spotting."

Pimiento cheese fell from Norma's mouth. "You have?"

I told them everything, excluding the part about the green eyes. I just didn't want to say that with Urleen around. Somehow it didn't feel right.

"Well, I'll be," Malene said. "Good. Rufus is around. So what are we going to do about it?"

I licked my lips. "We strike tonight."

Willard and Jack returned then, and we came up with a plan. It was messy, far from perfect, but it was the best plan we had and for the limited amount of time that we had, it was as good as things were going to get.

We finished eating and planned to all meet up that night, outside the church. I kept my fingers crossed that everything would be okay.

"You're not taking your hammer?" Lady asked later that afternoon.

"No, I'm most certainly not taking my hammer. With my luck it would fix something and in turn, would wind up breaking half the town."

"Oh yeah, I forgot about that."

I finished putting on my shoes and pulled Lady into a hug. "I'll be back later, okay. If something happens to me, know that I love you."

She smirked. "Ain't nothing gonna happen to you."

We didn't know that. "You're right. I'll be back before you know it."

"You sure will." I headed for the front door, and Lady called out, "Clem?"

"Yes?"

"I'll be praying for you."

"Thank you. We're going to need it."

Malene, Jack and I all hopped into Willard's truck. We were silent on the way to the church, not knowing what we would find, and worried about what we would.

I'd brought along a few orbs, but I was nowhere near ready for a battle. I wasn't Rufus. Warring against anyone wasn't my forte.

"Urleen and Norma Ray are going to meet us there?" I found myself whispering to Malene.

"That's right."

I nodded. "Okay. Sounds good."

After we hit every stoplight in town, we finally reached the church. The parking lot was full. Yep. Clark was going to move tonight, I had no doubt about that.

We found parking on the street a little ways away, and Malene called Norma Ray. When she hung up, she said, "They're walking up this way now."

The five of us joined up, and then I turned and faced the church. It seemed ominous as dark clouds formed above it and the wind blew the trees, sending brown leaves falling from their mostly green branches and hitting the cars.

The only thing we were missing was a bolt of lightning to strike above the church. That would've just been the cherry on top.

"What do you think we're in for?" Willard asked.

"A battle," Jack said dryly, "and one that we're ill prepared for."

"We can do it," Malene said. "I've got a few cards up my sleeve."

I hoped one of those cards included a way to defeat the enemy and send them back to Hades where they belonged.

The parking lot, though full of cars, was completely empty of people. For no good reason, I shivered as we passed a Buick.

"Should we go inside?" Norma Ray asked.

"Seems like we'll be putting ourselves at risk," I said. "We'll be in there with all those people, outnumbered and at their mercy."

"We'll stay out here," Willard said.

"And do what?" Norma Ray asked, hands on hips in defiance. "Use a bullhorn to get Clark out here?"

"Do you have one?" Jack asked.

Urleen opened her purse. "I'm sure I've got one in here somewhere."

It would have been funny if we'd been in any other situation. As it was, nothing was humorous about that moment.

But as it turned out, we didn't have to go inside or make any decisions about that because the doors swung open. And we all jumped back.

Clark stood between the doors. A throng of people were behind him, holding knives and looking very, very sinister. The light coming from the church haloed Clark and made him look like a demonic angel. I supposed that he just looked like a demon. There was nothing angelic about him—now that I knew the truth.

"You've made it," he said happily. "I'm so glad that more of God's children have come to join us."

"We haven't come to join you," Willard announced. "We've come to stop you."

Clark quirked a brow in amusement, which irked me. "Stop me? From what?"

"From hurting the good people of this town," I said.

Clark laughed. "No one wants to hurt you."

"You don't," Norma Ray said in surprise.

"No. We don't want to hurt you. We want to put you in your place, strip you of your power and show the world that magic is evil, that the only good place for it is taken out of this world." Clark gestured to the heavens. "The only power that we follow here is of the Lord God. He has given sanctity over all."

"He created us, too," I said.

Clark shook his head. "What goodness has come from magic? Those who have it use it for their own selfish purposes. Where is there a wizard who is healing people and letting the world know about it?"

"I'm sure there are plenty of doctors who do, they just keep that to themselves," I replied.

He tsked. "How naive of you, Clementine. You see, me and my people here, we've realized that magic is nothing but a blight on this town, in this world. We aim to get rid of it, to stop it for once and for all."

I took a step forward. "And did you tell them about your own use of magic?"

Clark didn't even stutter. "My gift comes from God himself. There is no magic in these hands."

"Then why don't you prove it," I challenged. "Heal someone."

He rolled his eyes. "Fine. I will heal someone. Who needs to be healed?" He turned around and pointed to someone. "You, there. Come here."

An older man with a severe limp stepped through the crowd to reach the door. My goodness, Clark should have healed his limp ages ago.

"In case y'all were wondering, he didn't want to be healed because he liked his limp and got it fighting in the war," Clark told us.

"Oh, I was wondering," Norma Ray said.

"That's why," he told us. "But now, it's time to do the healing. It's time to remove this limp from you and make you whole." Clark pressed a hand to the man's forehead. "By the power invested in me, I grant you healed by the word of God!"

Clark waited a moment and then let his hand drop from the man's head. "You are healed. Go and walk in the way that you haven't done in years."

The old man smiled, took one step. Took two steps and—limped.

Clark's jaw fell. "You should have been healed. Let me try that again."

So they went through the whole big show of praying and all that, and when Clark brought his hand away, the same thing happened.

"Looks like you lost your touch, Clark," Jack said.

The people behind the pastor started to murmur. It was Willard who stepped forward. "This man is not a prophet. He's not a healer. He's nothing more than a wizard, the same sort of person that he's been telling all of you to hate and to despise; he's been one of them this entire time. He's not even healing you. What he's done is performed glamours. Over time they will fade because they don't last long. They're nothing more than sleight of hand, a magician's trick. You've been conned by a conman who wants you to turn against your friends and loved ones. Well, we don't do that in Peachwood, do we? We stick by our friends. It's time that we showed him who we really are."

Clark was fuming. "I don't know what you did, but this isn't over yet. My army will fight for me, and so will my main soldier."

He lifted his hand toward the people, and they moved aside to let someone through.

I gasped as the person stepped forward.

Clark's lips pulled back into a malicious smile. "I believe all of you know Rufus, my lieutenant. Fight, Rufus, fight these people and destroy them."

CHAPTER 24

Behind Rufus, the rest of the people were stepping forward. "All of you," Clark commanded. "Fight them all. Destroy them!"

Oh crap. This was bad. We'd been expecting a fight, but I'd hoped to keep it contained to Clark and not have to battle half of Peachwood.

Yeah, I know, I was pretty naive, even though everyone had been suggesting that this exact scenario was what was going to happen.

Rufus marched forward, green eyes glowing. "I'll take him," I shouted. "All of you fight the rest of them."

Nothing about this was fair. I was sending a team of geriatric witches and wizards to fight a bunch of young men and women. Yes, some of them were old, but a lot of them were young.

"We're on it," Malene said, moving forward with a handful of orbs. "Try to save Rufus!"

She handed an orb to Urleen and one to Norma Ray, and they started fighting, throwing them at the knife-wielding army. The orbs were sucking up the knives, taking them from the people. When the knives were out of their grasp, the green flickering in their eyes died.

Yes! Something was working!

But before I had time to rejoice, Rufus advanced on me. He lifted his hand as I said, "Rufus, it's m—"

He hit me with a blast of magic that sent me skidding down the sidewalk. The force of the blast stole the air from my lungs, and I was sucking and heaving, trying to get the air back.

"Rufus," I said, coughing, and managing to get a word out, "it's me." I rose and he stopped to regard me. Good. That was progress. He wasn't just hitting me with magic. "It's me, Clementine. I've been so worried about you. Don't you remember what happened? We went to the cabin and saw Jody showing the knives to someone, and then we were discovered. You sent me back to Peachwood, but they captured you. They did this to you. Rufus, please!"

I was practically crying, begging him to hear me and for the green to leave his eyes. For goodness' sake, he wasn't even saying anything. It was like battling the Winter Soldier. He was all mission and no fun.

And I loved him! My heart ached as he lifted his hand to shoot me with magic again. Well, I'd been pretty roughed up the first time. I didn't want to go spiraling into the windshield of a car.

So I did the only thing that I could think of—I charged my body full of magic and raced forward, hitting my shoulder against his arm.

The force of my electrical charge sent him flying through the air. I winced as his back collided with a tree.

"Oh no! I've killed him!"

I raced to Rufus, hoping that he was okay. *Please, Lord, don't let me have killed him. Please let Rufus be okay.*

His eyes were closed when I reached him, and I leaned down to touch his face. His eyes popped open, and he touched my arm. A jolt of magic coursed through me, sending hot pain down my spine.

I kicked until he released me, and I shouted out to Malene, who was busy fighting over a knife that Claire held, "I can't break him out of the spell!"

"Keep talking to him," she shouted over her shoulder. "Snap him out of it."

"Snap out of it," I shouted to Rufus, who charged forward, hand outstretched, power churning in his palm.

I thought of all that we'd been through, of all the pain and anguish that he unleashed on himself, of all the turmoil that had led up to the point we were at, and I filled my body with it.

In a hand-to-hand fight, there was no way that I would win against

Rufus. He was simply too strong. I couldn't out-magic him, but I could out-emotion him.

That I was sure of.

I filled my body with thoughts of him, making it like electricity that snaked across my skin until I was supercharged with it.

Rufus neared and I opened myself to him, ready to either die or win this fight.

His hand struck me. The magic pulsed through my body like a tidal wave, and I fought back, pushing with all those thoughts, letting my magic touch his and shoving it back into him like a knife.

He bowed back and stumbled. The green light that had been flickering in his eyes sparked before sputtering out.

"Rufus?" I dared, breath clutched in my chest.

"Clementine," he whispered.

Tears pricked my eyes. "Yes, it's me!"

He rushed to me and swept me into a hug. Every emotion that I felt flooded from my arms—love, desire, comfort, joy—everything I had went into him.

He kissed me deeply, but not for too long because, you know, battle.

So many questions filled my mind. Like what had happened to him? How had Clark gained control of his mind?

"We need to destroy the weapons," he said as if hearing my question. "It's the only way to stop this."

"But how?"

"Easy," he said, a confident smirk on his face. "We do it one by one. Let's go."

We charged into the melee. Rufus used his magic to pull weapons from people's hands, and once the weapons were free, I zapped them with my supercharge powers, which caused them to explode.

Hey, whatever worked.

We did that over and over, but it felt like we weren't getting anywhere. There were so many weapons and so many people.

Just when I thought that I didn't have any energy left, Malene exclaimed, "They're here!"

I sneaked a quick glance over my shoulder and spotted a hundred or so witches and wizards, all of whom I recognized as being from Peachwood, making their way down the street.

"Destroy the weapons," Rufus shouted to them.

They sprang into action, and we all seemed to feel recharged, for we were hitting the people with everything we had.

Luckily, even though the fighting was going on our side, no one had been hurt. In fact, once a person's weapon was broken, Clark's power of them was destroyed and we told them to get out of the way so as not to get hurt.

That seemed to work pretty well and we were winning. Finally after what felt like hours, all the weapons had been destroyed and the only people left were Jody and Clark, who stood on the church steps.

Rufus strode up. "You've been defeated."

Clark's lips peeled back, making it look like he was growling. "You haven't won."

Rufus laughed. "Face it. It's over. Your attempt to sway Peachwood hasn't worked."

"He's right," Jody said. "I'm out of here."

He disappeared in a plume of smoke. But I didn't want Clark to get away so easily. He needed to pay for lying to the people of Peachwood, for swindling their hope from them.

In fact, as we stood there, I started to see everyone's aches and pains returning. I saw that Claire's hand had become withered again. Clark was losing his power. I wasn't sure if that was because he was on the verge of breaking emotionally or if his hold on the very people of Peachwood had shrunk because their belief in him had died, bursting into flames.

"I will win," Clark said.

"You will go to jail," Rufus told him.

He pulled an orb from his pocket and tossed it at Clark. A bubble formed around him, and Clark hit it, puncturing the bubble.

He jumped from it and said, "You will never catch me."

As Rufus lunged for him, Clark vanished through a portal, which closed behind him as quickly as he had stepped through it.

He was gone. We had won, but with him on the loose, it didn't feel like a victory. In fact, it felt very much like we'd still been defeated.

I exhaled a deep breath. "That wasn't how this was supposed to end."

Rufus shook his head. "That's because it's not over. Not by a long shot." He turned to the people. "Everyone. We can all go home now. It's over. Clark won't be returning to Peachwood anytime soon."

"But what if he comes back?" Claire asked. "What do we do then?"

"We fight him again," he told her.

"But he'll have learned. He'll be smarter."

"Then we just have to be smarter."

We were smarter, for not all of us had turned. Urleen had managed not to be swayed by the knife's spell. It was possible. But how had she not turned when Rufus had?

Well, I supposed some things were best left for the morning.

As people hugged and congratulated one another, my family and friends approached Rufus, ecstatic that he was with us once more.

"You had me so worried," I murmured on our way back to Willard's truck a short time later.

Rufus wrapped his arm around my shoulder. "You were worried? I was trapped and couldn't get free. I didn't want to fight you, but I had no choice. That's terrifying."

"But we made it," I told him.

He smiled sadly. "We did. And I hope never to be used like that again."

I hoped so, too.

CHAPTER 25

Things quickly returned to normal in Peachwood. To say that I was ecstatic that Rufus was back was the understatement of the year. He was happy as well.

We spent more time with one another. Like, a lot more time. He could be found most days at my house or me at his. We ate half our meals together and basically puttered around with one another (when neither of us were working, that was).

It was almost impossible to focus on work anyway because, well —Rufus!

He'd quickly told me exactly what happened (or what he remembered) about the night we went to the cabin. Jody had found him and took him to Clark. They decided to use one of the weapons on him to turn him to their side and control his mind. Rufus fought them, he remembered. But they increased the control of the weapon with magic until he succumbed.

Rufus and I didn't talk about the most obvious elephant in the room —that one of his fears, that he would turn evil, had come true. I don't think Rufus talked about it because it hadn't been his choice. He'd fought tooth and nail to remain himself. In the end I think he realized that what had happened to him could have happened to anybody.

"Urleen's on her way," I told him.

He was at my house. We'd just finished eating lunch, which consisted of chicken salad on lettuce and thick slices of Coca-Cola cake because you know how I felt about chocolate.

Rufus was wiping the last plate. He glanced up from his work and smiled. "Good. We've waited too long to do this."

We were taking the knife that Jody had given her and putting it away, someplace hopefully where no one would find it. Rufus was seeing to that. He didn't want to destroy the weapon, I think as some sort of reminder to himself of the sort of evil that existed in the world.

I would have been happy to toss it over a cliff and never see it again. But alas, what I wanted wasn't always what got done.

Urleen, as you remember, didn't wind up turning with the rest of everyone in Peachwood. We still didn't have a good explanation for that other than the fact that either the magic in her knife wasn't as strong as some of the other magic or Urleen's power was simply too strong, her will to remain good overcoming the evil.

Also she hadn't been cornered by two men and forced to submit like Rufus had been. He understood that and didn't let it get to him.

But it did get to him that Jody and Clark had escaped. We didn't know where they were. We'd tried several tracking spells, but nothing had worked. One thing we knew was that they would return. We also knew that we'd be ready—no matter what.

The doorbell rang a few minutes later, and Rufus gave me a big squeeze. "You ready?"

I nodded. "Sure am."

"Hurry up and answer the door," Lady said. "They may have food for me."

I smirked, but when I opened the door, Malene did indeed have a treat for Lady. She piled into my house along with Urleen, Norma Ray, Willard and Jack.

"You ready, son?" Willard asked.

Rufus nodded. He took the knife from Urleen and magicked up a portal. On the other side stood a man with long dreadlocks. His dark skin nearly shone from the torchlight that surrounded him.

"Erasmus," Rufus said, "this needs to go inside the Vault."

Rufus crossed the portal and handed the knife to Erasmus. "Thank you," Erasmus said.

He didn't ask any more about it. He simply regarded the knife and nodded, as if he knew all that it could do just by brushing his skin over it.

Rufus thanked him again, and he walked back to us and the portal closed behind him. "Well, that's done."

We were pretty quiet, all of us knowing we'd won the battle. But who would win the war?

It was Malene who broke the silence. "I'm glad that crap's over. Who wants to come back to my place for food?"

We laughed and folks started trickling across the street. Her normal sour mood had returned as soon as Clark vanished. She, along with everyone who'd been "healed," had become normal again. People were angry and resentful of what Clark had done. And wouldn't you know it, but just as soon as he'd left, Pastor Steve appeared asking what had been going on. It turned out that he'd been put under a sleeping spell and had been in bed for nearly two weeks.

We had all been glad to have him back. As Malene and everyone else wandered over, I turned to Rufus. "I know you're not hungry, but do you want to go over to her house?"

"In a minute. There's something I want to ask you first."

"Yes?"

His brow furrowed and my heart skipped. Was it bad? What was it that he had to ask me?

I waited, holding my breath, until he spoke. "When I came back, I realized how much I missed you. How much a part of my life you are."

"Oh, right. I know. The same thing happened to me."

He brushed a loose strand of hair from my eyes. "So I was wondering if you'd consider moving in with me."

My stomach dropped. Even Lady was silent. I could feel her gaze burning into me like a blowtorch. "Move in with you?"

He smiled. "Yes. I want us to be together. To move forward. So. What do you think?"

I opened my mouth, and the answer fell right on out.

～

Will Clem say yes? Find out in the next book, WHITE MAGIC AND WARDROBES. Click HERE to order.

Be sure to sign up for my newsletter so that you never miss a release. Click HERE to sign up!

Plus, join my private Facebook group, the Bless Your Witch Club. There you will receive sneak peaks at books, be the first to receive special giveaway offers and watch as I interview other authors that you love. But it's only available in the club, so join HERE.

And…I love to hear from you! Please feel free to drop me a line anytime. You can email me amy@amyboylesauthor.com.

ALSO BY AMY BOYLES

SERIES READING ORDER

A MAGICAL RENOVATION MYSERY
WITCHER UPPER
RENOVATION SPELL
DEMOLITION PREMONITION
WITCHER UPPER CHRISTMAS
BARN BEWITCHMENT
SHIPLAP AND SPELL HUNTING
MUDROOM MYSTIC
WITCH IT OR LIST IT
PANTRY PRANKSTER
HOME TOWN MAGIC

LOST SOUTHERN MAGIC
(Takes place following the events of Southern Magic Wedding. This is a Sweet Tea Witches, Southern Belles and Spells, Southern Ghost Wrangles and Bless Your Witch Crossover)
THE GOLD TOUCH THAT WENT CATTYWAMPUS
THE YELLOW-BELLIED SCAREDY CAT
A MESS OF SIRENS
KNEE-HIGH TO A THIEF

BELLES AND SPELLS MATCHMAKER MYSTERY
DEADLY SPELLS AND A SOUTHERN BELLE
CURSED BRIDES AND ALIBIS
MAGICAL DAMES AND DATING GAMES
SOME PIG AND A MUMMY DIG

SWEET TEA WITCH MYSTERIES

SOUTHERN MAGIC

SOUTHERN SPELLS

SOUTHERN MYTHS

SOUTHERN SORCERY

SOUTHERN CURSES

SOUTHERN KARMA

SOUTHERN MAGIC THANKSGIVING

SOUTHERN MAGIC CHRISTMAS

SOUTHERN POTIONS

SOUTHERN FORTUNES

SOUTHERN HAUNTINGS

SOUTHERN WANDS

SOUTHERN CONJURING

SOUTHERN WISHES

SOUTHERN DREAMS

SOUTHERN MAGIC WEDDING

SOUTHERN OMENS

SOUTHERN JINXED

SOUTHERN BEGINNINGS

SOUTHERN MYSTICS

SOUTHERN CAULDRONS

SOUTHERN HOLIDAY

SOUTHERN ENCHANTED

SOUTHERN TRAPPINGS

SOUTHERN GHOST WRANGLER MYSTERIES

SOUL FOOD SPIRITS

HONEYSUCKLE HAUNTING

THE GHOST WHO ATE GRITS (Crossover with Pepper and Axel from Sweet
Tea Witches)

BACKWOODS BANSHEE

MISTLETOE AND SPIRITS

BLESS YOUR WITCH SERIES
SCARED WITCHLESS
KISS MY WITCH
QUEEN WITCH
QUIT YOUR WITCHIN'
FOR WITCH'S SAKE
DON'T GIVE A WITCH
WITCH MY GRITS
FRIED GREEN WITCH
SOUTHERN WITCHING
Y'ALL WITCHES
HOLD YOUR WITCHES

SOUTHERN SINGLE MOM PARANORMAL MYSTERIES
The Witch's Handbook to Hunting Vampires
The Witch's Handbook to Catching Werewolves
The Witch's Handbook to Trapping Demons

ABOUT THE AUTHOR

Hey, I'm Amy,

I write books for folks who crave laugh-out-loud paranormal mysteries. I help bring humor into readers' lives. I've got a Pharm D in pharmacy, a BA in Creative Writing and a Masters in Life.

And when I'm not writing or chasing around two small children (one of which is four going on thirteen), I can be found antique shopping for a great deal, getting my roots touched up (because that's an every four week job) and figuring out when I can get back to Disney World.

If you're dying to know more about my wacky life, here are three things you don't know about me.

—In college I spent a semester at Marvel Comics working in the X-Men office.

—I worked at Carnegie Hall.

—I grew up in a barbecue restaurant—literally. My parents owned one.

If you want to reach out to me—and I love to hear from readers—you can email me at amyboylesauthor@gmail.com.

Happy reading!